The Ghost Road

Pat Barker

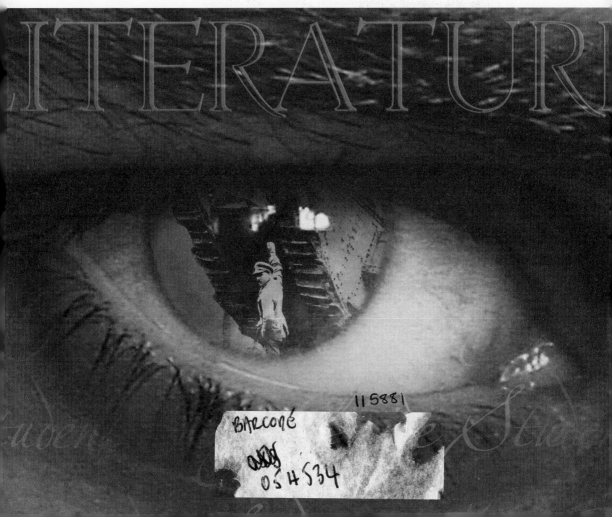

LITERATURE

Philip Allan Updates, an imprint of Hodder Education, part of Hachette UK, Market Place, Deddington, Oxfordshire OX15 0SE

Orders

Bookpoint Ltd, 130 Milton Park, Abingdon, Oxfordshire, OX14 4SB
tel: 01235 827720
fax: 01235 400454
e-mail: uk.orders@bookpoint.co.uk
Lines are open 9.00 a.m.–5.00 p.m., Monday to Saturday, with a 24-hour message answering service. You can also order through the Philip Allan Updates website: www.philipallan.co.uk

ISBN 978-0-340-96575-7

Impression number 5   4   3   2   1

Year 2013   2012   2011   2010   2009   2008

Front cover: detail reproduced courtesy of The London Illustrated News.

In all cases we have attempted to trace and credit copyright owners of material used.

Printed in Malta

Environmental information
Hachette UK's policy is to use papers that are natural, renewable and recyclable products and made from wood grown in sustainable forests. The logging and manufacturing processes are expected to conform to the environmental regulations of the country of origin.

Contents

Introduction

Aims of the guide

The purpose of this Student Text Guide to Pat Barker's award-winning novel, *The Ghost Road,* is to enable you to organise your thoughts and responses to the novel, to deepen your understanding of key features and aspects, and to help you to address the particular requirements of examination questions in order to obtain the best possible grade. It will also prove useful to those writing a coursework piece on the novel by providing a number of summaries, lists, analyses and references to help with the content and construction of the assignment.

It is assumed that you have read and studied the novel already under the guidance of a teacher or lecturer. This Student Text Guide is a revision guide, not an introduction, although some of its content serves the purpose of providing initial background. It can be read in its entirety in one sitting, or it can be dipped into and used as a reference guide to specific and separate aspects of the novel.

The remainder of this Introduction consists of Assessment Objectives, which summarise the requirements of the schemes of assessment employed by the various exam boards; revision advice that gives a suggested programme for using the material in the guide; and guidance on writing examination essays.

The Text Guidance section consists of a series of subsections that examine key aspects of the book, including contexts, interpretations and controversies. Terms defined in the 'Literary terms and concepts' on pp. 74–77 are highlighted the first time they appear in this section.

The final section, Questions and Answers, gives extensive practical advice about writing the various types of essay answer, and includes mark schemes, model essay plans and some examples of marked work.

Assessment Objectives

The AOs for A-level English Literature from 2008 are common to all boards:

AO1	articulate creative, informed and relevant responses to literary texts, using appropriate terminology and concepts, and coherent, accurate written expression
AO2	demonstrate detailed critical understanding in analysing the ways in which structure, form and language shape meanings in literary texts
AO3	explore connections and comparisons between different literary texts, informed by interpretations of other readers
AO4	demonstrate understanding of the significance and influence of the contexts in which literary texts are written and received

Revision advice

For the examined units it is possible that either brief or extensive revision will be necessary because the original study of the text took place some time previously. It is therefore useful to know how to go about revising and which tried and tested methods are considered the most successful for literature exams at all levels, from GCSE to degree finals.

Below is a guide on how *not* to do it. Think of reasons why not in each case.

Don't:
- leave it until the last minute
- assume you remember the text well enough and don't need to revise at all
- spend hours designing a beautiful revision schedule
- revise more than one text at the same time
- think you don't need to revise because it is an open-book exam
- decide in advance what you think the questions will be and revise only for those
- try to memorise particular essay plans
- reread texts randomly and aimlessly
- revise for longer than two hours in one sitting
- miss school lessons in order to work alone at home
- try to learn a whole ring-binder's worth of work
- tell yourself character and plot revision is enough
- imagine that watching the video again is the best way to revise
- rely on a study guide instead of the text

There are no short cuts to effective exam revision; the only way to know a text extremely well, and to know your way around it in an exam, is to have done the necessary studying. If you use the following six-stage method you will not only manageably revisit and reassess all previous work on the text but be able to distil, organise and retain your knowledge.

(1) Between a month and a fortnight before the exam, depending on your schedule (a simple list of stages with dates to display in your room, not a work of art), you will need to read the text again, this time taking stock of all the underlinings and marginal annotations. As you read, collect onto sheets of A4 the essential ideas and quotations. The acts of selecting key material and recording it as notes are natural ways of stimulating thought and aiding memory.

(2) Reread the highlighted areas and marginal annotations in your critical extracts and background handouts, and add anything useful from them to your list of notes and quotations. Then read your previous essays and the teacher's comments again. As you look back through essays written earlier in the course you should have the pleasant sensation of realising that you are now able to write much better essays than you could before. You will also discover that much of your huge file of notes is redundant or repeated, and that you have changed your mind about some beliefs, so the distillation process is not too daunting. Selecting what is important is the way to crystallise your knowledge and understanding.

(3) During the run-up to the exam you need to do lots of essay plans to help you identify any gaps in your knowledge and give you practice in planning in five to eight minutes. Past-paper titles for you to plan are provided in this guide, some of which can be done as full timed essays — and marked strictly according to exam criteria — which will show whether length and timing are problematic for you. If you have not seen a copy of a real exam paper before you take your first module, ask to see a past paper so that you are familiar with the layout, rubric and types of question. For each text you are studying for the examination you need to know exactly which assessment objectives are being tested and where the heaviest weighting falls, as well as whether it is a closed or open-book exam. It would also be helpful if your teacher shared with you the examiners' reports on past papers.

(4) About a week before the exam, reduce your two or three sides of A4 notes to a double-sided postcard of small, dense writing. Collect a group of key words by once again selecting and condensing, and use abbreviations for quotations (first and last word), and character and place names (initials). Choosing and writing out the short quotations will help you to focus on the essential issues, and to recall them quickly in the exam. Make sure that your selection covers the main themes and includes examples of imagery, language, style, comments on character, examples of irony and other significant aspects of the text. Previous class discussion and essay writing will have indicated which quotations are useful for almost any title; pick those that can serve more than one purpose. In this way a minimum number of quotations can have maximum application.

(5) You now have in a compact, accessible form all the material for any possible essay title. There are only half a dozen themes relevant to a literary text — though be aware that they may be expressed in a variety of ways — so if you have covered these you should not meet with any unpleasant surprises when you read the exam questions. You don't need to refer to your file of paperwork again, or even to the text. For the few days before the exam you can read through your handy postcard whenever and wherever you get the opportunity. Each time you read it, which will only take a few minutes, you are reminding yourself of all the information you will be able to recall in the exam to adapt to the general title or to support an analysis of particular passages.

(6) A fresh, active mind works wonders, and information needs time to settle, so don't try to cram just before the exam. Get a good night's sleep the night before so that you will be able to enter the exam room feeling the confidence of the well-prepared but relaxed candidate.

Writing examination essays

Essay content

One of the key skills you are being asked to demonstrate at A-level is the ability to select and tailor your knowledge of the text and its background to the question set in the exam paper. In order to reach the highest levels, you need to avoid 'pre-packaged' essays that lack focus, relevance and coherence, and that simply contain everything you know about the text. Be ruthless in rejecting irrelevant material, after considering whether it can be made relevant by a change of emphasis. Aim to cover the whole question, not just part of it; your response needs to demonstrate breadth and depth, covering the full range of text elements: character, event, theme and language. Essay questions are likely to refer to the key themes of the text, and therefore preparation of the text should involve extensive discussion and practice at manipulating these core themes. An apparently new angle is more likely to be something familiar presented in an unfamiliar way and you should not panic or reject the choice of question because you think you know nothing about it.

Read essay questions twice — the focus is not always immediately obvious. Many of them are several lines long, with several parts or sentences, some of which may be quotations from critics or from the text. You need to be sure of what a title is getting at, and the assumptions behind it, before you decide to reject or attempt it.

Different views

Exam titles are open-ended in the sense that there is no obvious right answer, and you would therefore be unwise to give a dismissive, extreme or entirely one-sided response; the question would not have been set if the answer were not debatable. An ability and willingness to see both sides is an Assessment Objective and shows independence of judgement as a reader. Don't be afraid to explore the issues and don't try to tie the text into one neat interpretation. If there is ambiguity it is likely to be deliberate on the part of the author and must be discussed; literary texts are complex and often paradoxical, and it would be a misreading of them to suggest that there is only one possible interpretation. You are not expected, however, to argue equally strongly or extensively for both sides of an argument, since personal opinion is an important factor. It is advisable to deal with the alternative view at the beginning of your response, and then construct your own view as the main part of the essay. This makes it less likely that you will appear to cancel out your own line of argument.

Although the essay question may ask you to base your answer on one passage, you should ensure that you also refer to other parts of the text. As long as you stay focused on your main selection of material and on the key words in the question, you will get credit for making brief comments on other supporting material, which could include reference to critical works, works by other authors, or other works by the same author, as well as links to elsewhere in the same text or selection.

Levels of response

A text can be responded to on four levels, but only the top one can receive the highest marks.

If you just give a character sketch or account of an incident this is the lowest and purely *descriptive* level, giving evidence of no skill other than being aware of the plot and characters, which does not even require a reading of the text itself. You are dealing only with the question 'What?', and in a limited context.

The next level, at about grade D, is a wider or more detailed *commentary* on events or characterisation, even making connections between them, but which still does not show real understanding of the text or an ability to interpret its themes.

For a C or low B grade you need to link different areas of the text, enter into *discussion* and explore major issues, though they may be in isolation from each other. This type of response addresses the question 'Why?'

A high B or A grade requires you to perform on an *analytical* level, showing an ability to think conceptually and to range across the whole text. You need to infer and draw conclusions based on an overview gained through a grasp of the overall themes that provide the coherent framework for the text. As well as character, plot and theme analysis, you will need to discuss language, style and structural elements, and link everything together. The question 'How?' is fully addressed at this level.

Length and timing

You will probably know by now whether length or timing is a problem for you. Although quality matters more than quantity, fewer than three sides of A4 writing makes it unlikely that you will have been able to fully explore and give a comprehensive answer to the question. On the other hand, you will typically have only one hour — minus planning and checking time — to actually write your essay, so you must practise the planning and writing stages under timed conditions until you are confident that you can give a full answer, ideally four sides, within the time limit. Finishing too early is not desirable, since the essay is unlikely to be as good as it could have been if the time had been fully utilised. The secret of length/timing success is to have developed a concise style and a brisk pace so that a lot of material is covered in a short space.

Choosing the right question

If there is a choice, the first skill you must show when presented with the exam paper is the ability to select the questions on the text that are best for you. This is not to say you should always go for the same type of essay, and if the question is not one that you feel happy with for any reason, you should seriously consider the other, even if it is not a type you normally prefer. It is unlikely, but possible, that a question contains a word you are not sure you know the meaning of, in which case it would be safer to choose the other option.

Don't be tempted to choose a question because of its similarity to one you have already answered. Thinking on the spot usually produces a better product than attempted recall of a previous essay that may have received only a mediocre mark in the first place. The exam question is unlikely to have exactly the same focus and your response may seem 'off centre' as a result, as well as stale and perfunctory in expression.

Underlining key words

When you have chosen your question, underline the key words in the title. There may be only one or as many as five or six, and it is essential that you discover how many aspects your response has to cover and fix in your mind the focus the answer must have. An essay that answers only half of the question cannot score top marks, however well that half is executed, and you need to demonstrate your responsiveness to all the implications of the question. The key words often provide the sub-headings for planning and can suggest the overall approach to the essay.

Planning and structuring

To be convincing, your essay must demonstrate a logical order of thought and a sense of progression towards a conclusion. If you reproduce your ideas in random order as they occur to you, they are unlikely to form a coherent whole. Jumping between unrelated ideas is confusing for the reader and weakens the argument. If you find yourself repeating a quotation or writing 'as I said earlier' or 'as will be discussed later', you have probably not structured your essay effectively. There is no right structure for an essay, as long as there is one.

When planning an essay — which you can afford to spend seven to eight minutes on — your first action should be to brainstorm all the appropriate ideas and material you can think of, in note form and using abbreviations to save time. You should aim for 10 to 12 separate points — about half a page — which will become the 10 or 12 paragraphs of your essay. If after a few minutes you do not have enough material, quickly switch to the other essay title. Beside each point, in a parallel column, indicate how you will support it. Next, group together the ideas that seem to belong together, and sort them into a logical order, using numbers. Identify which point will be the basis of your conclusion — the one with the overview — and move it to the end. The first points will follow from the essay title and definition of key words, and will be a springboard for your line of argument.

Remember that character, events and aspects of language exist as vehicles for a text's themes — the real reason why texts are written. You need to become accustomed to planning by theme, using the other three elements to provide support and examples. Material relating to social and historical context needs to be integrated into your response and not just tacked on to the beginning or end.

Your plan should be cancelled with one diagonal line when you have finished writing your essay. The examiner does not want to start reading it by mistake, but

will note that it exists and it will raise expectations of a good essay. Your plan can be flexible — you can add extra material or decide to delete some during the writing stage — but it provides your basic structure and safety net.

Evidence

When selecting a point, check that you can support it adequately and convincingly; if not, substitute a better point. Unsupported assertion does not get much credit in exam essays and gives the impression of desperation or lack of familiarity with the text. Using about three paragraphs to a page, you should structure each paragraph by making a point and then supporting it with textual evidence, and a brief analysis of what it contributes to the overall answer to the question; without proof, paragraphs will be undeveloped and insubstantial.

Support for your argument can take three forms: reference, example or quotation. Aim for a mixture of these forms, as well as of different kinds of evidence (character, plot, image etc.). Quotation is not a substitute for thought or argument; it should support your interpretation and relate directly to the point you are making. It is the most effective way of proving familiarity and confidence in the use of the text, and of validating your claims.

When using other people's ideas as support, you must give credit where it is due, rather than trying to pass them off as your own. It rarely fools the examiner and it is much more scholarly to attribute the reference, unless it is something that has been completely absorbed into your own interpretation and expressed in your own words. Otherwise, you can acknowledge source material by paraphrasing or summarising it, or by quoting exactly in inverted commas, mentioning the author in each case. A third option, if you have a quotation or idea you want to include but can't remember exactly where it came from, is to say 'as has been claimed by a critic' or 'it has been pointed out that…'.

Choose exactly the right quotation for what you are trying to prove, and use only the words from it that are appropriate. You can show that you have removed words from a quotation by using the ellipsis symbol (…) to replace the missing section. The cardinal rule is to quote accurately. If in doubt, it is safer to paraphrase than to guess wrongly.

Don't be afraid of using too much quotation; up to a quarter of an essay, or one per sentence, is acceptable. However, quotation for the sake of it, without interpretation or relevance, is useless, and you should aim for short integrated quotations of two or three words rather than longer ones, which take time and space. Short quotations (less than one line of printed text) can be incorporated into your own sentence; longer quotations need to be introduced by a colon and inset from both margins. If you are considering using such a lengthy quotation, pause and ask yourself if it is all necessary.

If you can't think of the right quotation to prove a point, reconsider whether the point is valid or worth making, or use an example or illustration instead. Remember that a quotation may prove more than one point; rather than repeating it, which weakens its effect, use it as a 'sandwich' between the two ideas it illustrates, which gives the impression of clever planning and structuring.

When making quotations, you do not need to give page references. Never give references instead of the quotation.

Put quotations in inverted commas; underline or use inverted commas for the title of the text.

Openings

Openings are the first indication to the examiner about whether you are an excellent, middling or weak student; it will be difficult to correct that first impression. By the end of the first paragraph you will have revealed an ability to write relevantly, accurately and clearly. For the most part, the best way into a literature essay is to define the implications and complexities of the title, starting with the underlined key words, especially if they are abstract concepts with a variety of possible interpretations (such as 'successful' and 'true'). Next, the widest and broadest application of the terms to the text will produce a range of ideas that could themselves be the structural headings for the essay.

As well as indicating the scope and framework for the answer, the introduction should provide brief and relevant contextual information. This may refer to the genre, the setting, the themes or the characters. It should not, however, be any of the following: a full plot synopsis; a summary of the life and work of the author; a repeat of the question; a vague and unfocused comment on life in general; or a list of any kind. Only points directly relevant to the question can be credited, so get started on the analysis as soon as possible. An introduction does not need to be more than a sentence or short paragraph and should never be longer than half a page.

Writing

With a useful plan you can write continuously — without needing to stop and think what to say next — and with fluency and coherence. You will need to write quickly and legibly. Think about appropriate expression and accuracy, always asking yourself 'What exactly am I trying to say?' Try to sound engaged and enthusiastic in your response; examiners are human and affected by tone as much as any reader is with any text. It is actually possible to enjoy writing an essay, even in exam conditions. Learn and apply the mnemonic acronym ACRID (accurate, concise, relevant, interesting and detailed).

Each paragraph should follow logically from the one before, either to continue the argument or to change its direction. Adverbial paragraph links — such as

'Furthermore', 'However', 'On the other hand' — are vital pointers to the progression of the argument. Paragraphs are a necessary courtesy to the reader and an indicator of point/topic change; paragraphs that are too long or too short reveal repetitive expression and lack of structure, or undeveloped ideas and lack of support respectively.

Avoid tentative or dogmatic statements, which make you sound either vague and uncertain or pompous and arrogant. Don't overstate or become sensational or emotional; steer clear of cliché and 'waffle'. Use accepted literary conventions, such as discussing literature in the present tense, using the surnames only of authors, and avoiding calling a reader 'he'. It is safer to stick to the text itself, rather than to speculate about the author's intentions or personal viewpoint. Examiners are not looking for evidence of what you know about the author; they want to see your response to the text and how you can apply your analysis to the question.

Write in a suitably formal, objective and impersonal style, avoiding ambiguous, repetitive and vague phrases. The aim is always clarity of thought and expression. Use appropriate technical terms to show competence and save words, and choose exactly the right word and not the rough approximation that first comes to mind. Remember that every word should work for you and don't waste time on 'filler' expressions (such as 'As far as the novel is concerned') and adverbial intensifiers (such as 'very' and 'indeed'). Say something once, explore it, prove it and move on; you can only get credit for a point once. You do not need to preface every point with 'I think that' or 'I believe' since the whole essay is supposed to consist of what you think and believe. Don't keep repeating the terms of the title; the whole essay is supposed to be linked to the title, so you don't need to keep saying so. It must always be clear, however, how your point relates to the title, not left to the reader to guess or mind-read what you think the connection may be.

Don't speculate, hypothesise, exaggerate or ask questions — it is your job to answer them. Feelings are not a substitute for thought in an academic essay; 'I feel' is usually a prelude to some unsubstantiated 'gushing'. Don't patronise the author by praising him/her for being clever or achieving something. Don't parrot your teacher. The examiner will quickly spot if the whole class are using the same phrases, and will then know it is not your own idea that is being expressed. To quote from examiners' comments, to achieve a grade A, candidates are required to 'show a freshness of personal response as opposed to mere repetition of someone else's critical opinions, however good'. Whether the examiner agrees with you or not is irrelevant; it is the quality of the argument that counts.

Whilst writing, you need to keep an eye on the clock and aim to finish five minutes before the end of the exam to give yourself checking time. If you find you are running short of time, telescope the argument but try to cover all your points; as an emergency measure, break into notes to show what you would have written. This is worth more than spending your precious last five minutes finishing a particular sentence but not indicating what would have come next if you hadn't miscalculated the time.

Endings

Many students have trouble with endings, which are as important as openings. They are what the whole essay has been working towards and what the examiner has in mind when deciding upon a final mark. An ending needs to be conclusive, impressive and climactic, and not give the impression that the student has run out of time, ideas or ink. An ineffective ending is often the result of poor planning. Just repeating a point already made or lamely ending with a summary of the essay is a weak way of finishing and cannot earn any extra marks.

There are techniques for constructing conclusions. You need to take a step back from the close focus of the essay and make a comment that pulls together everything you have been saying and ties it into the overall significance of the text. A quotation from within or outside the text, possibly by the author, can be effective and definitive. You can also refer back to the title, or your opening statement, so that there is a satisfying sense of circularity for the reader, giving the impression that there is no more to be said on this subject.

Checking

Writing quickly always causes slips of the mind and pen, and unfortunately these missing letters and words, misnamings of characters and genre confusions, are indistinguishable from ignorance and therefore must be corrected before submission. In addition, unchecked work will give a negative impression of your standards as a literature student.

Allow five minutes for checking your essay. Having spent several months on the study of a text it is worth getting your only exam essay on it as good as you can make it. A few minutes spent checking can make the difference of a grade. Don't be afraid to cross out; neat writing and immaculate presentation are not skills being assessed, but 'accurate and coherent written expression' is. As long as it is done neatly with one line, not a scribble, and the replacement word is written above legibly, correction counts in your favour rather than against you. Insert an asterisk in the text and put a longer addition at the bottom of the essay rather than try to cram it into the margin, where it will be difficult to read and is encroaching on examiner territory. If you have forgotten to change paragraphs often enough, put in markers (//) to show where a paragraph indentation should be.

When you check, you are no longer the writer but the reader of the text you have created, and a stranger too. Can you follow its line of argument? Are the facts accurate? Does it hang together? Is the vocabulary explicit? Is everything supported? Most importantly — but sadly often not true — does it actually answer the question (even if the answer is that there is no answer)? You also need to watch out for spelling, grammar and punctuation errors, as well as continuing until the last second to improve the content and the expression. Don't waste time counting words.

There is no such thing as a perfect or model essay; flawed essays can gain full marks. There is always something more that could have been said, and examiners realise that students have limitations when writing under pressure in timed conditions. You are not penalised for what you didn't say in comparison to some idealised concept of the perfect answer, but rewarded for the knowledge and understanding that you have shown. It is not as difficult as you may think to do well, provided that you know the text in detail and have sufficient essay-writing experience. Follow the process of **choose**, **underline**, **select**, **support**, **structure**, **write** and **check**, and you can't go far wrong.

Text Guidance

LITERATUR

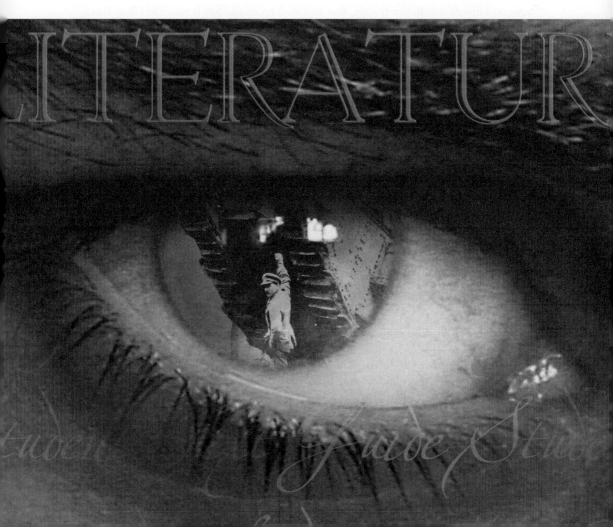

Contexts

Life and works of Pat Barker

Pat Barker was born in Thornaby-on-Tees in Yorkshire on 8 May 1943. She studied International History at the London School of Economics; she also studied at Durham University. Barker was encouraged to write by the novelist and short story writer, Angela Carter, but for a writer she was late in being published: her first novel, *Union Street*, was published in 1982, when Barker was 39. She seemed determined to make up for this delayed start: *Blow Your House Down* was published in 1984, *The Century's Daughter* in 1986, and *The Man Who Wasn't There* in 1989.

However, it was with the publication of *Regeneration* (1991) that Barker became known to a wider audience. It received widespread critical acclaim and was eventually made into a successful film. Its sequel, *The Eye in the Door* (1993), the second instalment in the trilogy, was also well-received, but it was *The Ghost Road* (1995) that won her the Booker Prize, which is generally considered the most prestigious literary prize in the UK. The First World War influences much of her writing: *Another World* (1998) contains a character who fought in the war, and her latest novel, *Life Class* (2007) is set in 1914 and is concerned with a group of artists who are coming to terms with the impact of the conflict. Other **themes** that dominate the *Regeneration* books occur in her other novels: in *Border Crossing* (2001) a psychiatrist is a central character again; and in *Double Vision* (2003) she returns to the subject of war, this time in a modern context, but with many of the searching questions about self-worth and guilt, so familiar from earlier works, dominating this work as well.

In 2008 *The Ghost Road* was included in the shortlist to decide 'the best of the Booker' prize winners, and although it did not win, its inclusion shows that it continues to be read, and to be highly regarded, by many people. Barker's reputation as a novelist is assured: each work forces the reader to think about difficult ideas in an accessible and highly readable **style**.

Barker has written that:

> I think there is a lot to be said for writing about history, because you can sometimes deal with contemporary dilemmas in a way people are more open to and because it is presented in this unfamiliar guise, they don't automatically know what they think about it, whereas if you are writing about a contemporary issue…sometimes all you do is activate people's prejudices. I think the historical novel can be a backdoor into the present which is very valuable.

> 'A backdoor into the present: an interview with Pat Barker' by Wera Reush

The last sentence is particularly interesting because it shows us how Barker views her text's relationship with the past: essentially, she claims, it acts as a lens through which

we can see the present more sharply defined, and this is nowhere more clearly seen than in *The Ghost Road*, a novel that seeks to present anew, and to modernise, a period of our history that is both familiar and distant.

Edwardian England

For many historians and literary critics, the modern age begins in 1914 with the outbreak of the Great War (for obvious reasons it was only known as the First World War after the Second World War). On reflection, this date signalled the end of many things: the class system was ruptured, the political classes were challenged, the military was almost completely destroyed, and some felt that inherited authority would no longer be able to rule unchallenged. Between the death of Queen Victoria (in 1901) and the declaration of war, Britain — and much of Europe — had enjoyed a *belle époque* (a beautiful era) — an optimistic time that produced great art, and when some enjoyed great privilege. The First World War fundamentally changed our view of history. As Geoff Dyer wrote in *The Missing of the Somme* (2001): '…the past *as past* was preserved by the war that shattered it. By ushering in a future characterised by instability and uncertainty, it embalmed for ever a past characterised by stability and certainty.'

Queen Victoria personified this complex time: she was austere, earnest, god-fearing, a devoted wife and a strict mother; she was also the self-confident, obstinate, materialistic, domineering queen of the British empire, the superpower of its time, and the politically astute advisor to six prime ministers (Lord Melbourne, Sir Robert Peel, the Lords Russell and Palmerston, Disraeli and Gladstone). If Victoria shaped her time then her son and heir, Albert Edward, perhaps unintentionally came to be closely associated with the time that he lent *his* name to: it was a period in which Britain emerged from the relative sobriety of his mother's reign into a more dissolute and, some might say, recognisably modern era of conspicuous consumption (it was the time when shopping as a leisure activity, rather than a necessity, was introduced to Britain by two Americans, Frank Woolworth and Gordon Selfridge). Queen Victoria epitomised a time of unprecedented British expansionism, and her passing marked, for many, the beginning of Britain's decline. The novelist Henry James summed up the thoughts of many when he wrote:

> I fear that her death will have consequences for this country that no man can foresee. The Prince of Wales is a vulgarian…The wretched little 'Yorks' are less than nothing…The Queen's magnificent duration has held things beneficially together and prevented all sorts of accidents.

Roy Hattersley, in his book *The Edwardians* (2004) noted that 'the persistent myth depicts the Edwardian era as a long and leisurely afternoon'. But it was also a time of profoundly important — and very modern — developments: the car and the passenger aeroplane made their full debuts; additionally, it could be argued that modern medicine began in this period, as did the modern political party system, the welfare state (through the introduction of the National Insurance Bill), and the media (especially newspapers and the cinema) increased in importance. The spirit of the age was one of invention, and that desire to innovate would be seen, with terrible effect, on the battlefields of France as the machine gun replaced the sword and the tank replaced the horse. It is, says Roy Hattersley, a myth to see the Edwardian period as 'a congenial bridging passage between the glories of the nineteenth century and the horrors of slaughter in France and Flanders'. The reality was very different.

Edward VII

Edward VII was the king of the United Kingdom of Great Britain and Ireland, and Emperor of India (1901–10). He was born on 9 November 1841, the eldest son of Queen Victoria and Prince Albert. He had a difficult childhood. His parents were determined to shape him into something that he clearly was not: namely, a young man with a fine academic mind. Although he attended the universities of Edinburgh, Oxford and Cambridge he did not excel. His interests were not cerebral; indeed, the older he got, the more distracted he became by drink, sport and women.

He married Alexandra, the eldest daughter of King Christian IX of Denmark, in 1863 and succeeded to the throne in 1901. Many view 'Bertie' (as he was affectionately known) as a buffoon, a drinker who disregarded his wife's feelings (he had a number of mistresses, including, most famously, the actress Lily Langtree). He is seen as someone who valued socialising more than his duties as the Prince of Wales and, later, king. This is not entirely fair. As head of state he travelled extensively, and he was undoubtedly influential in bringing Britain, France, Italy, Spain, Portugal and Germany together to sign an arbitration treaty in 1903–04. He was particularly instrumental in bringing Britain and France together in the *entente cordiale*, thus ending many years of suspicion and enmity between the two nations. Indeed, it probably did more than this: it helped persuade both nations that Germany, rather than each other, was the biggest threat.

Edward died at Buckingham Palace on 6 May 1910, having reigned for only nine years. He had three daughters and two sons. His second son George succeeded him to the throne and ruled the country until his death in 1936.

The fact that almost all of Europe's royal families were related to one another undoubtedly meant that their influence within political circles was profound and far-reaching. That this influence was so great speaks volumes for the influence of European monarchies: but such power being concentrated in the hands of unelected figureheads was to be another casualty of the Great War.

George V

King George V was crowned in Westminster Abbey on 22 June 1911. He was a politically astute, if somewhat dull, man. It was he who, in 1917, and in order to appease British nationalist feelings, changed the royal family name of Saxe-Coburg-Gotha to Windsor. It was the king who advised his then prime minister, David Lloyd-George, not to offer asylum to his first cousin, Tsar Nicholas II of Russia and his family, when the Russian revolution broke out in 1917. The Romanovs, George felt, might be an unsettling influence in Britain. They were shot soon after by revolutionary guards. Such actions suggest a ruthlessness which, given the uncertainties of the time, possibly helped save the British monarchy when many others in Europe were swept away by the forces unleashed by the war.

A changing society

At the beginning of the twentieth century Britain was still governed by men who had inherited their wealth from the land. But not for much longer. Britain had undergone an industrial revolution in the nineteenth century that had transformed urban and rural areas; but this process of change did not slow down with a new monarch. The census taken in 1901 shows that over 25 million Britons lived in urban areas (4.5 million in London) and 7.5 million in the countryside. By 1911, 41% of the population of England and Wales lived in London and the industrialised areas of the North and the Midlands. Population shifts continued to alter the demographic make-up of the country: this was the age of mass emigration to North America and Australia (at the peak, in 1912, 268,485 people left Britain for new lives abroad). The population was ageing too, which made the loss of an entire generation even more catastrophic.

Class

No discussion of any period in the history of Great Britain would be complete without class at its centre. The country had undergone a period of rapid industrialisation in the nineteenth century, and this brought previously unimaginable riches, as well as extreme squalor and deprivation. It is tempting to view the Victorian period through the often graphic but subjective lens of Dickens's prose, but although the Victorian ruling class was responsible for enforcing working conditions which, to a modern eye, are astonishingly cruel, it was also capable of change. By the end of the nineteenth century compulsory education for children was on the statute books, slavery had been abolished, public lending libraries and parks were established, paid holidays accepted, public transport, in the form of trams, buses, the underground and the most extensive rail network in Europe, were all widely available, making the late nineteenth century a period of remarkable mobility — both physical and social. This momentum sped up even more with the Edwardians.

Class, however, continued to underpin society at every level, as is evident throughout *The Ghost Road*, and especially when Billy Prior is the main focus of the **narrative**. The officer class was equally representative of the public school, Oxbridge-educated set of men who saw their power and status as a birthright. The First World War, among other things, forced these men to live and die side by side, and through this new intimacy it was obvious that the old divisions would have to be rearranged once peace had returned. It has been argued that the sense of duty that was so inculcated in the working man towards his social superiors made the sacrifices of the war more understandable; there were sporadic outbreaks of unrest, in the British, French and German armies but, given the conditions and the number of deaths, it is remarkable that only one large-scale rebellion occurred (in France in 1917). 'Never such innocence again,' said Larkin many years later, and he was right.

Work

Any society that undergoes such a rapid transformation is likely to see stark inequalities. The life of the average worker in Edwardian England was not a happy one. In 1911, 8.6% of the population of England and Wales was living two to a room, but in other areas the situation was far worse: in some parts of London it was 16.7%, and in the East End it was 36%. The author Jack London wrote in 1902:

> Nowhere in the streets of London may one escape the sight of abject poverty, while five minutes' walk from almost any point will bring one to a slum; but the region my hansom was now penetrating was one unending slum. The streets were filled with a new and different race of people, short of stature, and of wretched or beer-sodden appearance. We rolled along through miles of brick and squalor, and from each cross street and alley flashed long vistas of brick and misery.

Thousands were unemployed and homeless, and the hated workhouses were still operating, offering squalid conditions and the smallest amount of food and drink in return for back-breaking work. This overcrowding also was to be found in the expanding cities of the North and the Midlands.

Belle époque

But for many it was indeed a *belle époque*: this was an age of conspicuous consumption, a time when skilled workers, as well as Mr Pooter-like clerks and administrators, had more disposable income than they had ever had before. It was a time of a growing servant class, brought into being by the social aspirations of the new moneyed middle class. As they grew in affluence so they took flight from the crowded inner cities: they demanded new houses with gardens, away from the grime of the inner city, and it was this period that saw the growth of the suburbs. Those who wanted to shop in London could visit the new 'department store', Selfridges. They could pick up tips on how to furnish their newly acquired terraced suburban home by visiting the

Daily Mail Ideal Home Exhibition, established in 1908. This was an age of invention where one could look beyond the necessity for domestic staff and buy prototypes of the electric kettle, irons, washing machines and vacuum cleaners. A time was coming, it was hoped, when the machine would liberate people from the drudgery of labour, both at home and at work. The **irony** was that before that was to happen Europe would have to fight the first truly mechanised war. It was the age of the machine, but it would kill and maim just as much as it would liberate and transport.

World in motion

> The peaceful scene was changed, and with a blast of wind and a whirl of sound that made them jump for the nearest ditch. It was on them! The 'Poop-poop' rang with a brazen shout in their ears, they had a moment's glimpse of an interior of glittering plate-glass and rich morocco, and the magnificent motor-car, immense, breath-snatching, passionate, with its pilot tense and hugging his wheel, possessed all earth and air for the fraction of a second, flung an enveloping cloud of dust that blinded and enwrapped them utterly, and then dwindled to a speck in the far distance, changed back into a droning bee once more.
>
> Kenneth Grahame, *The Wind in the Willows,* chapter 2 (published in 1908)

The first tanks were introduced in the First World War: they transformed the later stages of the conflict, particularly on the Western Front around Amiens in 1917, where they were used especially effectively to punch through the German defences (anything that could cut through the miles of murderous barbed wire would almost certainly bring the stalemate to an earlier end). This was the deadly culmination of a period that had seen a true revolution in transport: the tank was the logical end to human endeavour, born out of desperation.

The Edwardian period was the dawn of an age obsessed with forms of transport that would transform the countryside and the city. The Victorians had laid the foundations of the most advanced railway system in the world, but the Edwardians added nearly 1,200 miles of track between 1900 and 1913. The age of the horse was in decline; but what replaced it was not any one, simple alternative form of transport, but many. The bicycle and the tricycle became common sights on the roads of Great Britain, with women in particular making great use of these cheap and fashionable alternatives to the expensive and unpredictable horse. The 'motor vehicle', 'horseless carriage' or, more commonly, the car (an Americanism that soon replaced 'carriage') underwent huge changes before it became affordable for a sizeable proportion of the middle classes.

Planes, trains and automobiles

Those who could not afford to buy a car had the choice of ever-faster methods of transport to get to work or to go on holiday. At the beginning of the twentieth century, in London alone, there was a profusion of different vehicles: one could travel by open-topped, horse-drawn omnibus, motor bus, (horse-drawn) hansom carriage, motorised taxicab or tram, and the rapidly expanding Underground system could quickly take you to your destination. Then there were the trains that brought in, and took out, the growing ranks of 'commuters'. The age that ended so savagely in 1914 was very much the 'golden age of steam': the railways opened up the country to hundreds of thousands of city dwellers who could use them because they were relatively cheap. Not surprisingly, class was integral even to this democratic method of transport, with the poorest members of society travelling third class, and the more affluent travelling first class.

The developments made on the ground were to some extent reflected in the sky. On 17 December 1903 the Wright brothers made history by successfully completing the first controlled, powered human flight in a machine that was heavier than air. The military took great interest in these developments, funding certain projects. In 1912 the Royal Flying Corps was founded, which was to become, in 1918, the Royal Air Force. Progress in both military and civilian terms of this method of transport was swift; again, the first dogfights between combatant aircraft took place in the First World War, as well as bombing raids on towns and cities. Aircraft, even more than the tank or the machine gun, would transform the nature of conflict and the tactics used by strategists.

Politics

Between 1902 and the outbreak of the First World War Britain had three prime ministers: these were (in order) Arthur Balfour (Conservative, PM from 1902–05), Sir Henry Campbell-Bannerman (Liberal, PM from 1905–08), and Herbert Asquith (Liberal, PM from 1908–16). Balfour and Asquith, although in many ways deeply conservative, began a process of constitutional change that would result in the Representation of the People Act of 1918. This abolished practically all property qualifications for men. Furthermore, for the first time it enfranchised women (but only those over 30 who met certain property qualifications). It was undeniably progress, but although men could vote from the age of 21, women were still not politically equal to men. Full equality would not occur for ten years.

It was obvious that the two Houses of Parliament were over-represented by the landed gentry, and just as there had to be profound changes in how the general population was educated if the country was to retain its position of power, it was clear that a new view of the nation-state was needed if the tensions between the classes were not to spill over into violence. The problem was that the Liberals and the Conservatives were both reluctant to cede too much power to women and the working class, forces that many in their parties viewed as dangerously subversive.

These (and other) forces for change were mobilising outside the Houses of Parliament, and writers such as George Bernard Shaw and H. G. Wells (those mentioned by Birling in J. B. Priestley's *An Inspector Calls*) were articulating for many the need for reform. Ramsey MacDonald became secretary to the Labour Representation Committee (the LRC) at the end of the nineteenth century; the LRC changed its name to the Labour Party in 1906, and in the same year MacDonald, along with 28 other MPs, was elected to the House of Commons to form the Parliamentary Labour Party. The Liberal Party had agreed a 'Progressive Alliance' with the Labour Party, which allowed the new party to put up candidates in seats without standing against Liberals. It was to prove a costly concession by the Liberals.

The rise of the unions

Organised labour — in union or party political forms — was gaining ground. Between 1910 and 1914 serious strikes broke out (among them the miners and the dockers), threatening to cripple the country's economy. They demanded better pay and working conditions. Between 1910 and 1911 the country was almost brought to a standstill by the unions, and there was a growing realisation that the more the ruling class depended upon the working man for his wealth, the more powerful the working man became: what he needed was organisation, and that came through the formation of the National Transport Workers' Federation. This laid the foundations for the Transport and General Workers' Union, founded in 1922.

The labour unrest that threatened to destabilise the country was not restricted to Britain alone. The ruling classes of the developed nations of Europe were terrified that the 'spectre' of communism would rock them to their foundations, and although the war stalled that (except in Russia), the high point of unquestioned, class-defined *noblesse oblige* was drawing to a close.

Education

It was not uncommon for the middle and upper classes to employ governesses or nurses to look after their young children. Edwardian families were rigidly hierarchical, with the father being the head of the family, the mother second, and the children very much their inferiors. The distance between adults and children is portrayed in *The Ghost Road*: Billy Prior is distant from both his parents, as indeed is Rivers, and even minor characters — such as Hallet — are seen as victims of a society that seemed determined to construct obstacles between the generations. To some extent we are led to believe that the psychic trauma experienced by many is a result of this emotional repression.

The Edwardians were by no means model parents but, it could be argued, they were more forward-looking than their forefathers: it was they who passed laws to register all midwives; the first nursery school opened in 1900; school meals were introduced in 1906; special schools for difficult and impoverished children opened in 1908; juvenile courts were introduced, as were borstals, and although these places were grim by modern standards they at least removed children from the danger of having to spend time in adult prisons. In addition, the first scouting camp was founded in 1907 by Lord Baden-Powell.

In 1902 Balfour's Education Act was passed. It was a revolution in the educational system, recognising as it did that if Britain was to remain a world power it could not expect to do so with an uneducated, illiterate workforce. The government created the model for the primary and secondary school system of education, which, like many other Edwardian inventions, was spread around the world through empire. However, most schools, whether grammar or private, remained brutal places, and the teachers employed in them were often uneducated and underpaid. Corporal punishment was routine, and it was a strongly held belief, certainly in the relatively privileged quads of the great public schools, that the duty of any school was to bend and shape the individual into an adult who was prepared to serve, whatever the service demanded. It was an attitude that would serve the country — if not the soldiers — well in the First World War, and it was neatly summed up in Sir Henry Newbolt's famous poem, 'Vitaï Lampada' (the lamp of life), a late Victorian poem that became hugely popular when war broke out.

To be young in Edwardian Britain meant having perhaps more opportunities than had ever existed before, but much was dependent on the class you were born into. There were opportunities to improve one's lot (literacy rose year on year in this time thanks to compulsory education and public libraries), but if you were working class it was almost inevitable that you would end up working in a physically demanding, low-paid job. If you were middle class (and male), however, the world was a different place: a good school, a place at university, a well-paid job: all these were possible, indeed, they were expected. But the war changed all that: the new world order, carefully engineered by men in hats, with thick moustaches and serious faces, was about to be violently shaken, never to return to what it once was.

Women

At the start of the twentieth century Britain was a patriarchal society. When one contemplates sepia-tinted photographs from this era, filled as they are with Larkin's 'fools in old-style hats and coats', what one sees are men dressed almost uniformly in black, and women dressed so that almost every part of their bodies is concealed. Each picture, to our modern eyes, seems to deepen our impression of an age characterised by sombreness and repression. Sexual expression, of course, finds its outlets regardless of the extent of the restrictions, and it was no different in the Edwardian period.

Before the First World War, 'women's work' was routinely domestic. Out of 24 million women, it is estimated that 1.7 million worked in domestic service, 800,000 were employed in the textile industry and 600,000 in various clothing trades, although the vast majority were expected to stay at home and look after the children and the home.

The British view of women was, at the outbreak of the war, recognisably Victorian: they were idealised, and seen as intrinsically good, incapable of violence, naturally supportive of men, protective, nurturing. A woman, according to *A Little Mother,* a popular pamphlet published in 1916, was 'created for giving life, and men to take it'. For the novelist Virginia Woolf, women had to act as magnifying mirrors 'reflecting the figure of man at twice its natural size. Without that power...the glories of all our wars would be unknown'. We see in countless visual and literary representations of women, creatures who were passive: they were urged to 'lie back and think of England' when having sexual intercourse with their husbands, a phrase that neatly sums up the relationship a woman was expected to have with both the man and her country. They were, when war broke out, and as countless propaganda posters show, used to blackmail their husbands and sons to behave 'like men': to go and fight, to not shame them by refusing to fight, to go and 'beat the enemy' in order to protect their wives, mothers and daughters.

However, much of this was to change when, because of the growing shortage of young men, women were called upon to do their work. Society seemed to accept these changes grudgingly, with some trade unions (organisations set up to protect workers' rights) suspicious that this new workforce would 'dilute' the trades they sought to protect. Nevertheless, women began to work, for the first time in Britain, alongside men in environments that were often aggressively masculine: they worked in munitions factories, steelworks, mines; they worked on the land harvesting crops, and they cared for the troops when they were sent home injured. Women were not granted the vote until 1918, and even then it was for those aged 30 and above, and suffrage was awarded as a way of thanking women for the contribution they had made to the allied victory. Even so, huge progress was made by women over the course of the war towards obtaining true equality in the eyes of the law.

The immense sense of loss the women experienced in these years — their beloved sons, brothers, husbands and fathers killed in seeing conflict — is beyond our imagination. Visit any war memorial in any British town or village and you will see the names of men from the same families killed, often within days of each other. Added to this was the trauma of adapting to the return of loved ones who had been injured, both psychologically and physically, by the war: it was often women who had to look after these men, many of whom had been altered beyond recognition by the battles they had fought.

The First World War

The First World War profoundly altered the world's political landscape and yet it is probably true that most people know surprisingly little about its causes. Sebastian Faulks summed up this opinion when he said in an interview with Margaret Reynolds and Jonathan Noakes (Vintage Living Texts) that 'people of my generation had rather my view: "terrible thing, appalling thing, massive slaughters… whew…you know…" but didn't really know much more than that'. It is also probably true that to some extent the First World War suffers in comparison with the Second World War. The later conflict is seen as a clear, black-and-white battle of ideologies: democracy versus dictatorship. Taking sides was, morally speaking, straightforward when one was facing the aggressive expansionism of Nazi Germany and Fascist Italy.

Our view of the conflict of 1914 to 1918 is very different: to some extent we see it as a terrible mistake, an avoidable tragedy brought about by a series of ill-advised alliances and prolonged by outdated, entrenched tactics drawn up by arrogant and distant leaders — the donkeys who led the lions. The slaughter in the fields of France and Belgium was so great that it is almost beyond comprehension. The statistics alone tell the story: the Allied forces (the Russian empire, France, the British empire, Italy and, eventually, the USA) lost an estimated 5.1 million men, and the Central Powers (Austria-Hungary, the German empire, the Ottoman empire and Bulgaria) lost some 3.5 million; taken together this works out at nearly 5,500 deaths every day. The Allied powers also had nearly 13 million wounded military personnel, the Central Powers 8.5 million; nearly 8 million were recorded as missing. Many towns and cities were ruined as the fighting swept across borders.

The origins of the war

How could this happen? What most people do know is that the assassination of Archduke Franz Ferdinand, heir to the Austro-Hungarian throne, by Gavrilo Princip, a Bosnian-Serb nationalist, on 28 June 1914, set in motion a series of events that would result, a few weeks later, in the outbreak of the world's first global conflict. The assassination resulted in Austria-Hungary declaring war on Serbia, which in turn dragged in the other powers who had signed alliances to protect each other's interests. There were other reasons for the war: the rise of nationalism in Europe made Princip's action more likely; the alliance system was inherently territorial and confrontational, and it could be argued that if Franz Ferdinand had not been murdered then another incident would have resulted in conflict sooner rather than later.

The major powers, especially Germany and Great Britain, had embarked on a rapid (and financially damaging) arms race, which again heightened the tension in Europe. Added to these factors was a scramble for overseas markets — in particular the Far East — which meant that economic growth had to be aggressively pursued, often with military 'protection'. Many — including Vladimir Lenin (who eventually led Russia out of the war) — believed that the economic system of the time was the principal reason for war: markets had to be protected at all costs. Consequently, the main European powers engaged not only in a battle for the domination of Europe but, as they were imperial powers, to extend their empires as well. There was also a great degree of pride involved in heightening this conflict: nobody was prepared to back down because to do so would be to risk national humiliation and economic hardship. There were old scores to settle as well: France wanted revenge on Germany for its annexing of the provinces of Alsace and Lorraine in the Franco-Prussian war of 1870; Germany wanted revenge on France for taking Morocco at the beginning of the twentieth century.

Germany's Schlieffen Plan made its expansionist aims clear to everybody — it was preparing to fight on both its western and eastern flanks. Integral to this plan was the quick defeat of France and Belgium (on its Western Front). Germany's decision to build a navy, which it hoped would threaten Great Britain's, was blatantly confrontational. France and Russia had similarly aggressive military plans in place, both of which included seizing German land.

Such a climate goes some way to explaining why the Austro-Hungarian government used the assassination for its own ends: it knew that the ultimatum given to Serbia, containing impossible demands, could not be met, and that the only possible outcome would be war. Serbia had an alliance with Russia; for the Schlieffen Plan to work Germany had to attack France and Belgium before Russia. It declared war on Russia on 1 August and, two days later, on France. Germany's leader, Kaiser Wilhelm II, ordered German troops to attack Belgium and then France; this in turn brought Great Britain into the war as a consequence of its treaty commitment to defend the independence of Belgium.

The first modern war

The First World War saw the introduction of new, lethal military devices. Barbed wire, machine guns, poison gas and the tank and were all employed with devastating effect by both sides. The war transformed the world. Oliver Stone wrote (*World War One: A Short History*, Allen Lane, 2007, p. 29) that:

> ...in four years, the world went from 1870 to 1940. In 1914, cavalry cantered off to stirring music...Fortresses were readied for prolonged sieges, medical services were still quite primitive, and severely wounded men were likely to die. By 1918, matters had become very different, and French generals had already devised a new method of warfare, in which tanks, infantry, and aircraft collaborated, in the manner of the German *Blitzkrieg* ('lightning war' of 1940).

As the numbers of casualties increased, both sides began to literally dig themselves into fixed positions: moving was too dangerous, and so a war of attrition became established. The more entrenched they became, the more static the fighting; any progress on either side came at a heavy price. The names of the battles have passed into a collective memory, acting as shorthand for mass slaughter: Passchendaele, Verdun, Albert, Vimy Ridge, Arras, Ypres and, most infamously, the Battle of the Somme. In this battle, which started on 1 July 1916, 1,508,652 shells were fired in the week before the assault began; the British army suffered over 57,000 casualties in one day, of which nearly 20,000 died. The maximum distance taken on the first day of fighting, at the village of Montauban, was 1,200 yards.

The war dragged on without any one decisive breakthrough. But in 1917 two events changed its course: first, the new Bolshevik government in Russia, led by Lenin, withdrew from the war. The treaty they signed continues to be controversial because it ceded Germany so much land. Germany gained massive areas of eastern Europe and was able to redeploy many of its troops to the Western Front. Second, pressure on the president of the USA, Woodrow Wilson, to enter the war came to a head when German U-boats sank seven US merchant ships over a short period of time. The Americans were finding it increasingly difficult to remain neutral. The USA was not the superpower it would later become but, even so, its declaration of war on the Central Powers, on 6 April 1917, had huge consequences: it was able to send millions of men to the Western Front, thus neutralising the benefits of German disengagement from the Eastern Front.

A turning point

The battle at Amiens drastically changed the direction of the war. Allied troops employed hundreds of new tanks to cut through the barbed wire set by the Germans. In one offensive they advanced seven miles in seven hours. Further south, several days later, at Albert, the German army was pushed back 34 miles in a matter of days; psychologically it was extremely damaging because they were back to their starting point of 1914 — the Hindenburg Line. In territorial terms they had achieved nothing.

American and Commonwealth forces were, by 1917, overwhelming German resistance (the USA alone was sending 10,000 men a day to Europe). Coupled with falling industrial output at home, the German forces' morale was very low, and the Allied forces capitalised on this with relentless assaults. Germany had no choice but to seek an end to the war: Wilson demanded the abdication of the Kaiser, and with it came the end of imperial Germany. With the defeat of Germany the Central Powers collapsed almost immediately: first Bulgaria, then the Ottoman Empire, and finally the Austro-Hungarian Empire, surrendered to the Allied forces. On the eleventh hour of the eleventh day of the eleventh month a ceasefire came into effect.

Peace — but not a lasting one

The Treaty of Versailles marked both the formal cessation of conflict and the end of four empires: the German, the Austro-Hungarian, the Ottoman and the Russian.

In purely political terms the most lasting consequences of the war were the enormous war reparations that Germany was forced to pay to the victorious powers; the nationalist movement led by the Nazi party exploited the overwhelming sense of grievance felt by ordinary Germans who saw that the ongoing, crippling financial burden would continue to hamper any hope of their country recovering from the terrible conflict. To add insult to injury Germany was forced to accept responsibility for the war.

The full consequences of the First World War can only be guessed at: we can look to the history books and see how countries emerged or died in this terrible theatre of conflict, and we can read about the effects the war had on those who took part in it through the many letters and poems written at the time. Ninety years on, it is still impossible to comprehend the impact of this first global war. Nothing can tell us of what we lost: the poets, musicians, artists, scientists and politicians, most unknown, who died before they had realised their full potential; or just the ordinary men who would, if they had lived, gone on to be good and caring fathers to children who now would remain unborn.

Many have argued that the causes of the Second World War can be found in the First World War: certainly it fostered in Germany a sense of resentment that made the rise of Hitler and Nazism possible. Hitler promised the German people a renewed sense of self-belief, and the desire to right the wrongs of Versailles meant that within the space of a generation the world was drawn, once again, into a devastating conflict.

The history books can only do so much; it is for the artists to give voice to those names that now collect moss and lichen; it is for writers to make their characters as real to us as possible; in that way we can, hopefully, begin to understand the losses felt by those involved in the conflict.

Trench warfare

To-night, His frost will fasten on this mud and us,
Shrivelling many hands, puckering foreheads crisp.
The burying-party, picks and shovels in shaking grasp,
Pause over half-known faces. All their eyes are ice,
But nothing happens.

The last verse of 'Exposure' by Wilfred Owen

Many men joined up at the start of the war because they were promised that it 'would all be over by Christmas'; they also perhaps visualised a war of 'derring-do', dashing about on horseback, or shooting the Germans from a safe distance. It was impressed upon them that to fight was their duty, but the dangers involved were both concealed and, to a great extent, unknown. There were added attractions and incentives: many joined the army because they were promised that they would serve alongside their friends and work colleagues (these became known as the 'Pals

Battalions'); many also joined because it provided some regular pay and an escape from the drudgery of their work. General Sir Henry Rawlinson, who was in charge of the British IV Corps at the outbreak of war, rightly argued that more men would volunteer if they knew the people they were going to fight alongside. Large groups of men from places as diverse as dockyards and public schools formed distinct battalions. The tactic was, in many ways, a resounding success: by the end of September 1914 over 750,000 men had enlisted; by January 1915 it had risen to 1 million. Out of nearly 1,000 battalions formed between 1914 and 1916, two-thirds were Pals Battalions. But the cost to local communities when these men were killed was huge.

Think of the war and we think of the trenches. Trench warfare began in September 1914 and ended in 1918. This partly explains why the war dragged on for so long: there was little movement from either side, and what movement there was came at great cost, as battles like the Somme and Ypres show. Men had to survive not only the bombs, bullets and gas attacks of the enemy but, as any reading of their diaries and letters home testifies, they also had to withstand appalling weather conditions as well as infestations of rats and parasites.

Disease, especially trench fever, which was similar to influenza, was spread by lice. They bred in the seams of uniforms and the soldiers complained of constant itching. Worse, though, were the rats. These flourished in the mud, water and waste: they fed on the corpses, in turn spreading disease; they ate through vital rations; they even nibbled through communication wires, putting the men at the Front at even

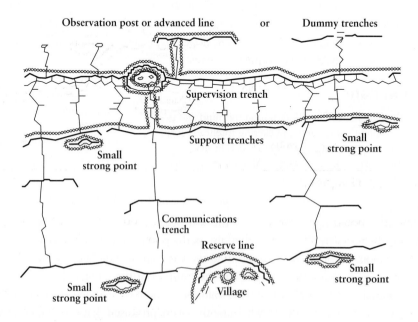

A typical trench system from 1916

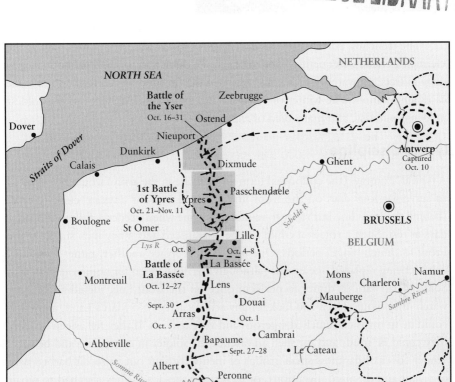

The Western Front, 1914

greater risk because they were cut off from HQ unless they repaired the damage. Diseases such as dysentery spread because of the poor hygiene: toilet facilities were basic and the buckets used often spilled into the trenches. Men often simply relieved themselves in shell holes, consequently infecting the water supply.

The rations that the field kitchens provided were, as the war dragged on, often barely enough to keep a man alive: biscuits, corned beef, tea, some bread and jam. This was the staple diet of the British Army and almost none of it was fresh.

The trenches, particularly the British ones, which were not as well built as the German trenches, frequently flooded. The men often had to stand for hours waist-deep in freezing water, which could result in the dreaded trench foot and in some cases amputation. The winter of 1916–17 in France and Flanders was the coldest in living memory, and many died of exposure.

Duty and discipline

A typical 'Tommy' (the **colloquial** term for a private in the army) would be expected to serve for four days on the front line followed by four days in 'close reserve' (behind the front line but ready to reinforce the line when needed), followed by four days at rest. Such a rotation could not be guaranteed and many men stayed at the Front for much longer periods. One unit would replace another, rather than individuals being replaced one by one (although this did happen for numerous reasons). Soldiers had various duties to perform once on the front line, including keeping watch: they would listen and look for any activity across No Man's Land, a job that could be in turns extremely dangerous and very tedious. If they fell asleep on duty they could be tried, and for such an offence the soldier in question could be shot. Under cover of darkness small groups of men were sent out to repair barbed wire (a recent and despised invention), or to recover the dead. They also had to repair the crumbling trenches. Each company of men had a commanding officer to whom they would report every hour, and it was his job to ensure that the rota of work was being enforced and that his men were prepared to attack or respond at short notice. All those on the front line had to wear their equipment at all times, with bayonets fixed. No man could leave his post without permission from his commanding officer.

The British Army was ruthless in maintaining discipline, and numerous charges brought against a soldier could result in the death penalty. The table below gives some examples of charges and penalties from the war.

Charge	Penalty
Doing violence to a person bringing provisions to the forces	Death
When acting as a sentinel on active service, sleeping at his post	Death
Striking a superior officer	Death
Committing an offence against the person of a resident in the country in which the soldier was serving	Death
Leaving the ranks on pretence of taking wounded men to the rear	Penal servitude
Leaving his CO to go in search of plunder	Death
Misbehaving before the enemy in such a manner as to show cowardice	Death

Those who survived the war did so by adapting to these outlandish conditions: they established routines, made friends, sang songs, played football, wrote letters home, read books and newspapers (which could be delivered by special request), kept pets (including rats), embroidered, smoked cigarettes, told jokes, went on leave back to 'blighty' (England) and got drunk; they even tried to make their trenches homely, giving them place names such as Lovers Lane, Lavender Walk, Idiots Corner, Chaos Trench, Gangrene Alley — each showing a bleak but necessary sense of humour. They did everything they could to remain human, and it is often surprising to see how 'normal' life was for many of them. Perhaps the most famous episode of mankind's willingness to resort to a familiar routine — despite the circumstances — came on Christmas Day 1915 on the Western Front. In some of the trenches there was a spontaneous outbreak of peace, with soldiers from both sides ceasing hostilities: they clambered out of their trenches, exchanged cigarettes, drank cognac, ate, joked and even played football together. The commanding officers were worried, however, that such informal truces would lower morale and soon ended such activities: they argued that it is harder to kill somebody you know than it is to kill a stranger.

The British Army

Although Great Britain was a global power at the end of the nineteenth century, its army was surprisingly small. Successive British governments had poured money into the Royal Navy rather than its land forces, believing that the empire could only be protected through naval power. Until the Germans began their programme of military expansion, the British remained detached from Europe, maintaining that the empire was the first priority. As the clouds of conflict began to darken the European skies it became increasingly clear that the old dependency on sea power, important though it was, would have to change, and that resources would have to be directed into the army. The unexpectedly difficult and prolonged Boer War, which the British had won but at tremendous cost, both in human and financial terms, exposed a land force that could be beaten by a relatively unsophisticated (but highly motivated) enemy.

The British Army, which numbered about a quarter of a million troops, was a professional force, and it was supported by several hundred thousand reservists and members of the territorial forces. Even so, it was no match for German land forces. With the outbreak of war, numbers had to expand rapidly if the British were going to help the French stop Germany. By 1915, 29 new divisions had been added to the existing army's forces, bringing in over 2 million more soldiers; in 1916 conscription was introduced, which added an additional 2 million men. However, the British, like their European counterparts, had to adjust to the new tactics being employed on the battlefields of Belgium and northern France: the horses that had

served in the Boer and Crimea conflicts would be either shot down by the new machine guns or snarled up in barbed wire. The First World War, more than anything else, forced the British Army to become a modern fighting machine.

The structure of the army

The British Army was (and is) made up of divisions and brigades — tactical units that can change depending on circumstances. Each brigade consists of battalions from different regiments, and these are far more permanent in nature. The regiment is the single most important unit in a soldier's life: each is responsible for recruitment and training, and many of the regiments have their own traditions dating back, in some cases, centuries. In the First World War whole battalions were recruited from the same geographical areas, which meant that there was a recognisable regional identity to each regiment, and this in turn contributed to the *esprit de corps*, so important in difficult circumstances. The main drawback to this was that if a regiment lost a lot of men — as happened in both world wars — local communities were devastated because the losses were concentrated in one area.

The British Army was engaged in active service for the whole of the First World War, and for much of that time it was entrenched in the Western Front. However, British soldiers fought in every area of the conflict, suffering heavy casualties. Few doubt the bravery of the 'Tommy' (as the British soldiers were called) in this conflict, but had it not been for the support of forces from Commonwealth and empire countries, not to mention the USA, the British would not have been able to stop the march of the highly trained German forces. At the outset of the war Kaiser Wilhelm had dismissed the British Army as 'contemptible'; at the end of the war its reputation had been transformed and it was viewed as a formidable opponent, but this had been achieved at great cost. Germany would not underestimate Britain again.

The war in brief

1914

- 28 June   assassination of Archduke Franz Ferdinand in Sarajevo
- 23 July   Austro-Hungarian ultimatum to Serbia
- 28 July   Austria-Hungary declares war on Serbia
- 1 August   Germany declares war on Russia
- 2 August   German ultimatum to Belgium
- 3 August   Germany declares war on France
- 4 August   Germany invades Belgium. Britain declares war on Germany
- 10 August   Britain declares war on Austria-Hungary
- 23 August   Japan declares war on Germany
- 7 November   British forces land in Mesopotamia
- 25 December   unofficial truce between British and German soldiers on the Western Front

1915

- 7 May — the *Lusitania* passenger liner is sunk off Ireland, with 1,200 lives lost
- 23 May — Italy declares war on Austria-Hungary
- 31 May — London attacked from the air by German Zeppelins
- 1 June — women employed by British munitions factories for the first time
- 6–9 August — Anzac offensive at Gallipoli
- 25 August — Austro-German forces capture Brest-Litovsk
- 23 September — Bulgaria joins the war in support of the Central Powers
- 25 September — Battle of Loos, a Franco–British offensive against the Germans, begins
- 6 October — Austro-German forces invade Serbia
- 8 October — Austrian forces capture Belgrade
- 11 October — Bulgarian forces invade Serbia
- 19 December — Evacuation of Allied forces on Gallipoli

1916

- 25 January — introduction of conscription in Britain for single men (extended to married men on 16 May)
- 21 February — Battle of Verdun — a key German offensive — starts (and ends on 18 December)
- 31 May — Battle of Jutland — the major naval battle of the war — begins
- 1 July — Battle of the Somme begins (and ends on 18 November)
- 27 August — Romania joins the war in support of the Allies
- 7 December — David Lloyd George replaces Asquith as British Prime Minister

1917

- 11 March — British forces capture Baghdad
- 12 March — Russian Revolution begins
- 15 March — Tsar Nicholas II abdicates
- 3 April — Lenin returns to Russia with help from German forces
- 6 April — USA declares war on Germany
- 31 July — Battle of Passchendaele begins (and ends on 10 November)
- 6 November — Clemenceau becomes French Prime Minister
- 15 December — Russia signs armistice with Germany

1918

- 1 April — creation of the RAF
- 7 April — meat rationing introduced across Britain
- 8 August — Battle of Amiens begins
- 21 August — Battle of Albert begins

- 3 November   Austria-Hungary signs armistice with the Allies
- 9 November   Kaiser Wilhelm II abdicates
- 11 November   Germany signs armistice with the Allies

The literature of the First World War

> The Great War, with its carnage of ruling class rhetoric, put paid to some of the more strident forms of chauvinism on which the English had previously thrived...[literature] represented a search for spiritual solutions on the part of the English ruling class...[it] would be at once solace and reaffirmation, a familiar ground on which Englishmen could regroup both to explore, and to find some alternative to, the nightmare of history.

> Terry Eagleton, *Literary Theory: An Introduction* (1983), p. 30

> However the world pretends to divide itself, there are only two divisions in the world today – human beings and Germans.

> Rudyard Kipling in *The Morning Post*, 22 June 1915

> If any question why we died,
> Tell them, because our fathers lied.

> Rudyard Kipling

In political terms Europe was relatively stable between the end of the Franco-Prussian War (1871) and the outbreak of the First World War. The majority of the growing middle class enjoyed a period of unparalleled prosperity at this time. Although the working classes of every industrialised nation probably did not view it the same way, the hardships experienced in the rapid process of industrialisation were, for many at the beginning of the twentieth century, starting to bring rewards. Businessmen travelled across Europe by train, and there was little bureaucracy to worry about. Behind this new openness, however, lay the organised unrest promoted by the European trade union movement, which was campaigning for better pay and conditions for the working class. Although the war interrupted such agitation in many countries, it erupted into revolution in Russia in 1917 and threatened to spread elsewhere.

It was in the arts that the *belle époque* found its lasting legacy. In art this period saw the growing acceptance of Impressionism, and later Expressionism, both of which were partial rejections of the romantic and conservative artistic schools of the nineteenth century. Painters such as Monet and Degas experimented with materials as well as methods, and this desire to reinvent and re-present the physical world so that it was seen to be to a great extent a projection of individual perceptual experience would reach its apogee in the Modernist movement of postwar Europe. In literature, writers such as Maupassant and Zola in France, and H. G. Wells, Henry James, Kipling, Conrad and Shaw in Great Britain, described the age in new and challenging ways.

Rudyard Kipling was perhaps Britain's most famous writer of the time. He was an ardent supporter of the war — the sort of person Owen was attacking in 'Dulce Et Decorum Est'. Kipling predicted the conflict and did his best to alert the country to the prospect of war with Germany, but his words went unheeded. When war was finally declared he was determined that his son, John, would enlist to 'do his bit'. John was underage and extremely short sighted, and was rejected several times, but Kipling used his influence to get the young man enlisted in the Irish Guards. Tragically, the day after his eighteenth birthday, John was killed in the Battle of Loos and his body was never recovered.

This was a shattering experience for Kipling, and a turning point in his writing, which takes on a new darkness after the war. In his short story, *The Janeites* (1924), Kipling shows an acute understanding of the military, and especially of the infantrymen who suffered so much, but he also explores how literature can be used not only to expose military and social conflict, but to escape from misery as well.'

War poetry and Owen

It is the poetry of the First World War that remains its most enduring literary legacy. The works of Sassoon, Rosenberg, Edward Thomas, Rupert Brook and, perhaps most famously of all, Wilfred Owen, define a generation's experience of this conflict. Owen's poetry is visceral in its power: seething with controlled rage, graphic in its descriptions of the scenes he saw at the Front, but always instilled with an acute intelligence that avoided simplistic and reductive negative propaganda. Owen's poetry is great literature in its own right.

He wrote many memorable poems — 'Anthem for Doomed Youth', 'Exposure', 'Futility' and 'Disabled' among them, but perhaps his most famous poem is ' Dulce Et Decorum Est'. The poem consists of 28 lines, written in a rather loose iambic pentameter. It describes a gas attack on a group of soldiers and the rush of the men to protect themselves from this new form of warfare. One in their number drops his mask, and the image of him 'guttering, choking, drowning' powerfully describes his painful death. The final lines of the poem, 'Dulce et decorum est/Pro patria mori', addressed to the propagandist Jessie Pope, confront 'the old lie' used to persuade young men to risk their lives: namely, 'it is sweet and fitting to die for one's country'.

Owen's poem was published posthumously in 1920. He was killed on 4 November 1918 — exactly one week before the signing of the Armistice — attempting, with the rest of his 'D' company, a crossing of the Sambre-Oise Canal at Ors. He was 25. He was promoted to the rank of lieutenant the day after his death; to add even greater sadness to this terrible episode Owen's mother received notification of his death as the church bells were ringing out to mark the end of the war. His poetry continues to be studied because it has real literary merit, but also because it articulates an authentic voice from the trenches: Owen — like Sassoon

— knew what the war meant, and as such it carries greater resonance, in many ways, than the work of those who wrote about it from a distance.

The First World War novel

For any writer — novelist, poet, historian or critic — who wishes to write about the First World War (or the Great War as it was referred to at the time) there is one obvious problem: how do you make your work original and distinctive? The conflict of 1914–18 was unusual for many reasons. First, the casualties were unprecedented and remain almost impossible to comprehend (over 15 million are estimated to have died). Second, it was the first truly modern war: tanks, aeroplanes, machine guns, barbed wire, gas, landmines — the ghastly litany of familiar methods of destruction were tested in the fields of northern Europe in this conflict (hence the appalling loss of life) and they have stayed with us ever since. The First World War was also the first war covered by what we now know as 'the media': it was the first conflict to be filmed (for reasons of propaganda as much as reportage). War correspondents sent reports back to their papers via telegram and war photographers captured action on the Front. It also inspired literature of unprecedented intensity and quality. In the age of satellite television, the internet and mobile phones we are used to watching conflicts as they unfold, but the First World War saw the beginnings of this process: we are familiar with the poetry of writers such as Sassoon, Owen, Brooke and Rosenberg (among many others), but behind them there is a wealth of photographic, aural, oral and written records that threaten to overwhelm — and to some extent invalidate — all subsequent voices.

First-hand accounts

Henri Barbusse's novel *Under Fire* was published in 1917 (and translated into English in 1918). It is one of the first novels of the conflict and was based on Barbusse's own experiences and set entirely in France. It is unflinching in its description of life in the trenches. It influenced Owen and Sassoon, and is regarded by many as a classic of the **genre**. Geoff Dyer, in *The Missing of the Somme*, quotes the following passage as particularly important because it looks ahead to how the war will be remembered — as well as forgotten and changed — by subsequent generations:

> We shall forget!…Not only the length of the big misery, which can't be reckoned, as you say, ever since the beginning, but the marches that turn up the ground and turn it up again…we shall forget not only those, but even the foul wounds of the shells and machine-guns, the mines, the gas, and the counter-attacks. At those moments you're full of excitement of reality, and you've some satisfaction. But all that wears off and goes away, you don't know how and you don't know where, but there's only the names left.

Remembering those names, if not the lives and experiences behind them, becomes a duty for a nation that promises, every November, that we 'shall never forget'.

Novels are part of that attempted, ongoing remembrance, and the writer can do much to fill in the blanks. Rebecca West's short novel *The Return of the Soldier* was published in 1918 (and set in 1916) and raises the difficult subject of shell shock: Chris Baldry returns to England suffering from amnesia and is looked after by three women he once loved. Jenny, his cousin and narrator, articulates a deeply held lament for a lost innocence and, indeed, a lost England.

Perhaps the most famous novel of the period is Erich Maria Remarque's *Im Westen nichts Neues (All Quiet on the Western Front)* published in 1929 (translated into English in 1930). It described the war (from a German perspective) in unflinching detail, and it became an international bestseller and an acclaimed film. It is narrated by Paul Bäumer, a 19-year-old writer and critical of the campaign and the damage it did to both individuals and society: at its heart is an exploration of the growing sense of dehumanisation the soldiers feel as they are caught up in a process they are unable to influence.

Remarque's novel is unusual because, unlike many of those written at the same time, it continues to be read and studied today. Another such novel is *A Farewell to Arms* (1929) by the American novelist, Ernest Hemingway. Again, like so many novels written about this period, it is semi-autobiographical. The story is narrated by Lieutenant Frederic Henry, an American ambulance driver serving in the Italian Army in the First World War, who falls in love with Catherine, a nurse. At its heart the novel is a love story, set against the backdrop of the war.

Second-hand accounts

So graphic and lastingly moving are many of these first-hand accounts of the trenches that one has to ask what can possibly be added to our understanding of this conflict by writers who did not experience it first hand. To put it simply: why read Pat Barker when one can read Wilfred Owen and Edward Thomas? It is not an easy question to answer, but it is worth considering since what art form other than literature can unify so many experiences into one narrative? The many voices of the First World War are individual perspectives and, as such, are fragments of an impossibly complex picture. A writer can attempt to bring many of these together and seek to present the personal and the political.

A writer can only hope to deepen our understanding of this thoroughly documented war if he or she is able to bring something new to the subject, and Barker does just this by adding a distinctly modern emotional and psychological force to existing narratives. The *Regeneration* trilogy is informed with the lessons of history, and presents the subject matter with the seriousness it deserves without avoiding asking difficult questions about the nature of war and the effects it has on society and individuals. It could be argued that those who are outside the tumult, but living with the consequences of the war, are as entitled to explore and interpret it as those who took part.

The resurgence of interest in the First World War novel in this country can be attributed to Pat Barker and Sebastian Faulks. Barker's trilogy (*Regeneration*, 1990, *The Eye in the Door*, 1993, and *The Ghost Road*, 1995) coincided with Faulks's *Birdsong* (1993).

Modernism and Freud

Modernism has no clear definition or period. One reason for this is that it was not a movement restricted to one genre: it ranged across literature, music, art and architecture and was, in many ways, a response to a variety of political and economic events in many different countries. Added to this, Modernism reached different peaks at different times within these countries: indeed, it could be argued that it was the dominant cultural tendency in France between the 1890s and 1940s, and the same could be said about Modernism in England from the beginning of the twentieth century and Germany from the 1890s to the 1920s. Different periods could be applied to Modernism in the USA and Russia. Roughly speaking, though, Modernism lasted in Europe between 1890 and the outbreak of the Second World War (in 1939). **Postmodernism**, which is as difficult to define as Modernism, is a term more often encountered after this date, but it would be a mistake to assume that with the 'rise' of Postmodernism Modernism was superseded: they coexisted (if they can be comfortably distinguished at all, which many critics question).

The First World War complicates the picture still further: some believe that the fragmentation of society that the war precipitated increased the momentum of Modernism; others believe that the war interrupted and possibly even derailed its development. To add further complications to any one clear definition, one has to accept that within such a loosely termed movement are other movements pertaining to different periods, including Surrealism, Formalism, Structuralism, Dadaism, Existentialism, Expressionism, Futurism, Symbolism and Vorticism, to name but a few. What we can say is that Modernism marked a break with the past: each artist who contributed to the movement questioned the established rules, and they often did so by using innovative **forms** of expression. It would have been impossible to imagine the Victorians understanding the literary forms explored by, among others, T. S. Eliot and James Joyce, although the origins of more abstract — and less **figurative** — art forms can be found in artists of the nineteenth century (most notably Turner and Whistler). Modernist artists in art, literature, music and architecture, could trace their influences back to the nineteenth century and beyond: it is a domino theory of effect. The difference was that they deliberately subverted many of the rules they had absorbed in order to represent a changed world in a way that reflected its new condition. As the Oxford English Dictionary states, Modernism can be 'generally characterized by a deliberate break with classical and traditional forms or methods of expression'.

Many factors influenced Modernism, most obviously new research in psycho-analysis and the politics of the left, especially that of Marx and Engels. It would, for example, be impossible to fully appreciate the theatre of Bertolt Brecht (1898–1956) or the art of George Grosz (1893–1959) without an understanding of the political context in which they worked: politics, economics, philosophy, psychoanalysis, all contributed to make the period before and after the First World War uniquely combustible.

Sigmund Freud

One figure who had a lasting and radical effect on mankind's view of himself is Sigmund Freud (1856–1939). A distinction must be made here between psycho-analysis (a term that Freud coined) and literary psychoanalysis. In modern novels such as Barker's *Regeneration* trilogy, characters are clearly viewed through the lens of modern psychoanalysis, and frequently explicitly so, but this was not necessarily the case at the time the novels were set. Modern writers and readers in the West live, to varying degrees, with a legacy of **Freudian** thought.

Of particular interest when studying the literature of this period are Freud's theories of the ego, the super-ego and the id. Freud developed the concept of a 'psychic apparatus' in 1923, which was late in his career. He felt that the human psyche could be divided into these three parts: the uncoordinated and impulsive urges can be termed the 'id'; the 'super-ego' represents the ideal and is inherently moralistic; the 'ego' balances these two extremes, and is often manifested in the individual's behaviour: it is realistic and organised. It is relatively easy to apply such concepts to nations as well as individuals, especially when we view something as extreme as the war. The id was described by Freud in the *New Introductory Lectures on Psychoanalysis* as 'the dark, inaccessible part of our personality'; it is child-like, and a child is dominated by the id. The action of taking a nation to war can be seen as an expression of the id: aggressive and short-termist, an outward expression of the uncivilised. The ego, 'what may be called reason and common sense', attempts to reign in the id. The ego is the conscious self, the part that is aware of the madness of the id and is able to judge it, control it, plan it and synthesise it with the super-ego. It is the super-ego that acts as the conscience; it provides the ideals, the goals, the (often unconscious) inherited models we as individuals and as a society reach for. The First World War, like all wars, can be seen as a massive externalisation of an inner conflict: the id running rampant before the ego can assert its sense of order. Applying Freud's concepts to literature can be illuminating, and in much of the literature of the First World War the characters described can be seen to be fighting with inner demons that neatly correspond to the id, ego and super-ego.

Freud's influence on modern Western thought is immense. The poet W. H. Auden wrote, in an obituary poem, that 'to us he is no more a person/now but a whole climate of opinion/under whom we conduct our different lives:/Like weather he can only hinder or help'. Auden's contention is that Freud irrevocably changed our way of looking at ourselves and each other: the language, references, images, interpretations — nothing relating to our emotional lives remained untouched by Freud. Indeed, experience itself, be it in extreme form (as in neurasthenia or shell shock) or something more prosaic, can be understood through Freudian psychoanalysis. Undoubtedly though, Freud's influence has declined, perhaps more in the field of psychoanalysis than in academic and cultural spheres; the work he did exploring the subconscious self continues to be relevant to many today, even those who have not read Freud himself.

Chapter summaries

Part one

One

The novel opens on a beach in the north of England (we later discover it is Scarborough). Billy Prior is watching the businessmen and families relaxing in the sun. One family — a mother, child and grandmother — attracts his attention. He exchanges a few words with the older woman and begins to think about returning to his barracks for his medical. On his way he sees some young men, both workers in the local munitions factory, and a young child holding some candy-floss. He begins to think about what he might have done if he had not signed up to fight: he, too, could have worked in a munitions factory, but he had decided not to do so, against his father's wishes. He is deep in thought as he walks back to his barracks, thinking of Charles Manning's offer of a desk job in the Ministry of Munitions (which he also rejected), and of Wilfred Owen.

At the medical the Medical Officer, Mather, a tough Scotsman, questions him about his asthma. Prior says that he only has asthma attacks at home, never at the Front. He was sent home for shell shock, suffering from mutism. Mather notes that W. H. R. Rivers treated Prior in Craiglockhart, and that he had a 'paralytic stammer'. Prior admits that he got into the army by lying to the doctor, and Mather comments that almost everyone seemed to do the same at the start of the war. Mather also suggests that Prior has 'done his bit', but Prior wants to return to action. He leaves Mather and walks over to the Appeals Board rooms. There he meets Owen and they talk about Sassoon's injury. After more questions about his asthma, Mitchell, the officer in charge, draws the hearing to an end with a non-committal comment about the likelihood of Prior returning to France.

Two

The scene changes to Ward Seven of a hospital for war casualties. It used to be a children's hospital, and crude copies of Sir John Tenniel's illustrations of *Alice's Adventures in Wonderland* still adorn the walls. Elliot Smith, a patient, asks Rivers if it is true that he knew Lewis Carroll and Rivers says that he did, although they were not close.

Behind the screens lies Ian Moffet. He claims that he is paralysed from the waist down, but Rivers is not convinced. Moffet collapsed on hearing the guns for the first time; when he woke up he could not walk. Rivers tells him that he is going to draw stocking tops on Moffet's legs and, over two weeks, will 'roll' them down his legs, drawing new lines, and with each advance feeling will be restored.

Rivers begins to think of Lewis Carroll (he uses Carroll's real name, Charles Dodgson). He remembers that Dodgson hated snakes and that, one day, when Rivers was young, he and his family took Dodgson for a walk and encountered a snake on the path. Dodgson had collapsed in fear, and his father threw the snake away. He also recalls another incident, filled with phallic symbolism, when his sister, Katharine, sat on an adder and ran home screaming. Rivers had tried to kill it in the hope of dissecting it later on, but when he tipped it out on the family hearthrug he discovered that it was still alive. His father and Dodgson stamped on it until it was dead.

After leaving Moffet (who is already beginning to believe that Rivers's unconventional treatment might work) Rivers continues to think of Dodgson, a man who, like Rivers, also had a very pronounced stammer; he also recalls how the elderly writer could not 'keep his hands off' the young boy, but that nothing developed beyond this. As Rivers grew up he began to see himself as the rabbit from *Alice's Adventures in Wonderland*, always disappearing down corridors consulting his watch. He admits to himself that he does not know himself very well; indeed, he seems to know his sister better than himself.

He recalls one episode in his childhood clearly: when Dodgson was asked about children one suppertime he said that although he loved all children he also felt that boys were 'a mistake'. Later, Rivers's mother reassured him that this was not the case, but the words stayed with him, and he wonders how Dodgson could prefer girls to boys.

He turns his thought to Geoffrey Wansbeck, a young soldier who has murdered a German prisoner of war. This patient has started to suffer from hypnagogic hallucinations, and now regularly visualises his victim. Wansbeck describes how he killed the German, but that he felt no guilt or remorse. Rivers notices that although his patient is very well-built and strong he is, nonetheless, broken in some way. Wansbeck believes he can smell something unpleasant, even though he knows it is psychosomatic. Rivers talks to Wansbeck about his condition and decides that he

would be better off going to bed. The chapter concludes with Rivers thinking back to his childhood once again, reflecting on Dodgson's words and concluding, in his childhood stutter, that boys are rough and noisy, and have to fight sometimes.

Three

Billy Prior is going back to France in a few days, and he has returned to the beach to contemplate his future (as well as his past). It is now all but deserted. Suddenly Prior is disturbed by a cry of pain: a red-haired woman has hurt her ankle because of her high heels. Prior immediately thinks she is a prostitute. The woman is offended that he thinks this, but says that he won't get 'it' for free, and these words start Prior thinking of another prostitute — Long Liz — who had sex with him out of her 'patriotic duty'. Brought back to the present day by the woman (Elinor) they walk off together to her room. They begin to undress, but Prior stops himself when he smells some gas and it transports him back to the trenches and terrifies him. The description is sordid: there is pubic hair and possibly semen on the sheets and the whole encounter is devoid of sexual excitement. As he begins to mount her things get even worse: he looks at her face and thinks back to when he, too, was being assaulted, this time as a child, by Father Mackenzie, his teacher. We also learn that Prior had been a prostitute of sorts, charging adults who wanted sex with him. Eventually he reaches a climax with Elinor, but only when he feels that he hates her.

He walks back to the barracks, passing some drunken soldiers on the way. He goes into his tent and remembers that Hallet, a young officer who is going to the Front for the first time, is sharing it with him. He is naive, even admitting to 'really rather looking forward to it'. Looking at him, Prior begins to speculate about life and death, and the random nature of both; he thinks that we are simply 'ghosts in the making', waiting to die. He realises that in 'trench time', when a generation lasts six months, he is old, and that Hallet is, in effect, his great-grandchild by comparison.

Four

Moffet continues to improve as the 'stockings' are erased and then re-drawn by Rivers. Moffet compares Rivers to seventeenth-century witch finders, and Rivers concurs, saying that both were looking for something 'abnormal'. Both men briefly discuss the nature of hysterical disorders and Rivers thinks that Moffet is too intelligent to accept his solution to Moffet's problem. This makes Rivers think of his time spent in Melanesia as a young anthropologist. He thinks of Njiru, a man who suffered from terrible curvature of the spine, and to whom he became particularly close because he was the local doctor. Rivers remembers how on one occasion Njiru attended an old woman, Namboko (meaning 'widow') Taru, who was apparently constipated. Njiru massaged her and relieved her of her pain. Njiru and Rivers discuss the nature of illnesses, or *tagosoro* as Njiru's people call them.

Moffet is improving but Wansbeck is not: he has a temperature, and Rivers suspects he might have influenza. Rivers continues to contemplate the loss of life: it is autumn, and the leaves in London are turning gold. Another patient — Major Telford — is convinced that a nurse has cut his penis off and pickled it in a jar of formaldehyde. He is clearly delusional and Rivers makes little headway with him. The experiment with Moffet continues, and with (outwardly at least) notable success: it seems that the drawn-on stockings have removed his hysterical paralysis, and he is even able to take a few steps on his own. But Moffet has not improved psychologically, and soon after this he is found in the bath, after drinking half a bottle of whisky and slitting his left wrist. Telford and Rivers, with great difficulty, get him out of the bath. He is still alive, and is quickly patched up by Rivers and the nursing staff.

Rivers's contemplative mood continues: the clicking sound made by the beads at the end of a blind takes him back, once again, to Njiru's Melanesia. He recalls going to some skull houses where Nareti, the mortuary priest, lived. The skulls and bones rattled in the wind, but before Rivers can think much longer about it he is brought back to the present day by the lift arriving.

Five

Billy Prior is sitting with his fiancée, Sarah Lumb, in her mother Ada's dining room. The Lumbs are respectable and solidly working class, but the God-fearing Ada does not allow the young couple out of her sight. Cynthia, the recently widowed sister, is also there, as is the vicar, the Rev. Arthur Lindsey. The latter, Prior notes to himself, is obviously homosexual, and blushes when Prior rubs his leg under the table. Prior himself is keen to make love to Sarah, but even though she visits him alone late at night she is reluctant to concede to his wishes for fear of being discovered by her mother.

The next day the family attends a spiritualist gathering (the 'spuggies'). Prior is unable to listen to much of the service and leaves quickly, followed soon after by Sarah. They hurry home where they quickly make love behind the sofa, only for the contraceptive to come off Billy inside Sarah. No sooner have they recovered themselves than Ada enters the house. The next day Sarah and Prior say goodbye; their proposed marriage has been met with astonishment by his parents, who consider Sarah — a common factory girl — beneath him. Prior recalls that his father had come to see him off the last time he was home, but it was an episode wreathed in a funereal atmosphere. And now, as he prepares to say goodbye to Sarah, they both watch as the pigeons — **symbols** of freedom — fly out as the train that will take Prior to the Front enters the station.

Six

Rivers is visiting his sister Katharine in Ramsgate. The town has been heavily bombed and, as a result of the worry, Katharine is in poor health. They look through old photograph albums together; the conversation turns to Dodgson again, and Katharine draws a comparison between her brother and the writer: both are loners. Then we are transported back to Rivers's childhood, and he is in the company of Dodgson again, this time waiting with his family for his sister to return. Dodgson is reading from *Alice's Adventures in Wonderland,* but just as he begins Katharine rushes in and presents him with some wilting flowers. He takes her onto his lap and continues reading.

Rivers thinks of the different course his life has taken from that of his sister: whereas his life has spread outwards into the world, her horizons have gradually shrunk to a bed in a small house in a small English provincial town. Katharine bemoans the fact that all the drawings and correspondence that they had from Dodgson have been lost, but she also mentions that a painting of their Uncle Will, which used to hang at the top of the stairs, went missing at the same time. It was of a grim subject: it showed their uncle having his leg amputated with a cauldron full of tar standing nearby to pour over the stump. She remembers that Rivers hated the picture. Suddenly Rivers, who has no visual memory, thinks bitterly that his father has, despite his efforts, failed him.

He later reflects on the painting. Rivers was named after Uncle Will, who shot the man who had shot Lord Nelson. Will Rivers had been severely injured in the battle, but he had survived the amputation and gone on to have a family of his own. Rivers remembers that, on one occasion at about the age of four, he embarrassed his father by crying in the barber's shop; his father slapped his leg, and then held him to compare him to Uncle Will, claiming that *he* had not cried, so why should Rivers? From that moment on he had a stammer. He also remembers Prior's words: namely, that Rivers had put his 'mind's eye out rather than have to go on seeing it'. He is forced to confront this suppressed memory.

He returns to London and meets Prior. There is some tension between the two, but Prior admits to being relieved to be going back to France that night. Prior talks about meeting Robert Ross, a friend of Sassoon's, and the sexual humiliation he had inflicted on a young man called Birtwhistle, who used derogatory terms to describe the working classes. Such people, Prior claims, are the reason he is leaving the country. The two men discuss the football being played between the British and the Germans in No Man's Land. They say farewell, and Rivers recalls that on one of his expeditions — in Vao — it was a custom for an illegitimate child to be raised as the son of one of the most powerful men in that society. At a given ceremony that child was ruthlessly killed by the stepfather. He thinks of a church in Maidstone, which has in its window Abraham about to sacrifice his son, and a ram caught in the thicket. This differs from the first scenario because God is present, and is about to stop the killing. He watches Prior go to France, another sacrifice.

Part two

Seven

The date is 29 August 1918, less than three months before the end of the war. The narrative position has changed: the text is now written from Billy Prior's perspective, and it has become more personal. The journal does not start from when we last saw him, just as he is boarding the train to London, but predates it by some weeks, and so we get more detail on Birtwhistle and others. Charles Manning, an officer with whom he has had occasional and casual sex, meets him off the train, and they go to a room he rents in Half Moon Street. Prior drinks some whisky and has a bath and they then have sex, with Prior becoming sexually dominant. They then go out to dinner and meet Birtwhistle, who proceeds to insult the working class. (It is worth noting here that Noel Pemberton-Billing was a British Member of Parliament who became preoccupied with the idea that homosexuality was infiltrating society during the First World War. Lord Alfred Douglas, once Oscar Wilde's lover, testified in Billing's favour when he was taken to court for accusing the actress Maud Allan of being a lesbian who was conspiring with those who wished to corrupt the country's morale. Billing defended himself and won.) Prior and Manning have sex again back at the rented room, but they are almost like strangers, with great distances opening up.

Prior buys an expensive coat and eventually leaves for the train station; Manning sees him off, but there is little warmth between them. Prior arrives in Folkestone, exhausted.

The next day Prior decides to go for a swim in the sea, which exhilarates him. It makes him think of a time on a beach in Scotland when he made love to Sarah. He writes to her once he has returned to his hotel, and then by chance meets Hallet with his family: his family are saying a long goodbye to him.

On the boat going over to France Prior remarks on the card playing, as well as the stormy weather and the terns flying slowly nearby. He talks to Hallet, who he describes as 'full of idealism', and is again contrasted with Prior's pragmatic fatalism.

At Étaples, a brutal training ground that prepares the new arrivals for the war, Prior is struck by the impersonal nature of all the relationships. He is with Hallet again, and they spend the night exchanging thoughts about their fiancées back home.

A few days later — on 7 September — Prior is preparing to leave to go to the Front. He notices that everyone is spending their last night writing — poems, letters, journals — and he thinks that they are doing so in an attempt to gain some immunity from death.

Eight

After walking on Hampstead Heath, Rivers returns home to bed feeling ill. A chance sighting of a photograph of his landlady's departed son starts him thinking of Melanesia and Dodgson again. He thinks of croquet with Dodgson, and he notes that because he can actually visualise the croquet lawn of his childhood he must be hallucinating. His memory slips into his time on board a ship taking newly 'missionised' natives from one Melanesian island to the next. He recalls talking to some of these people, and they remarked on the very obvious cultural differences between them. He begins to think that it is increasingly difficult to say that one culture is better than another, and that no God exists to pass judgement in any way. Without a God society is in 'free fall'.

Still in bed Rivers begins to think of the characters he met in southeast Asia at this time, aboard small boats and tramp steamers: Brennan, Father Michael and Hocart, each very different but each symptomatic of the economic, religious and cultural imperialism of the time. Brennan is an alcoholic trader in search of natives to sell and goods to trade with. He is the living embodiment of a culture with no moral high ground exploiting another — he is vulgar, misogynistic, and in stark contrast to the young Hocart and missionary Father Michael.

One evening, when the boat was moored near the Bay of Narovo in Eddystone, a man in early middle age approached Rivers and introduced himself as Njiru. Rivers noticed his curved back, but also — by Melanesian standards — his height, as well as his 'hooded, piercing, intelligent, shrewd' eyes.

We learn that Njiru was the eldest son of Rembo, the chief who controlled the most important cults on the island. Njiru was powerful because he had knowledge. Rivers discovered that the culture he was becoming intrigued by was sexually liberated, and when he met an elderly man who had had sex with every woman on the island there was a bonding between the men that crossed both cultures.

Rivers observed a newborn baby, motherless because her mother died in childbirth, struggling to hold on to life herself. He watched Njiru ask the mother's spirit to leave the child, to not haunt her, to let her live. Rivers discovered more about the ghosts of this culture, and later he talked to Hocart about the link between sex and death on the island. Hocart complained that for his research he would like more sex and less death.

Rivers next observed the death of Mbuko, in the company of Njiru and Rinambesi. Njiru tried to exorcise the ghost taking Mbuko's spirit, but when he died his body was carried out on a pole to the canoe where it was propped up in the sitting position and paddled out to sea, then unceremoniously thrown overboard. Hocart and Rivers were disappointed: they had hoped to see whether the natives might cut Mbuko's head off and keep his skull, but his was not a good death, or an appropriate death for head-hunting.

Nine

Prior is on the train going to the Front. The atmosphere is very masculine: full of lewd stories and rude jokes, but Prior is on the margins of these groups. It is cold, and the rain is beating down outside. The men get off the train and walk past ruined houses. Prior, Hallet, Owen and Potts are shown to an empty house where they can stay for a short while. With its lace curtains it is a strangely suburban setting.

The next morning the sense of strangeness continues. It seems as if the war has forgotten them, and the four men go about creating a 'fragile civilization', which approximates to something domestic. They argue about the war, with Hallet stating that it is a just cause. They collect discarded items, drink wine, and luxuriate in not fighting, or being momentarily released from the 'beast' of war.

Within this chapter Barker switches again to Prior's first person narrative. It is 11 September. Prior suspects that Owen is not happy that he is here, perhaps because of their shared history at Craiglockhart. That said, both men seem to have more in common with each other than Potts and Hallet because they are experienced soldiers. Two incidents show this: the first occurs in town when they witness some wounded soldiers going past (Owen and Prior are indifferent to it, Potts and Hallet are shocked), and the second involves Hallet catching some wasps on flypaper: Prior cannot stand the sound of dying and hurls it away. Prior thinks of the soldier who is waiting on him (Longstaffe): a former actor who imitates soldiering — rather like something out of *Henry V* — instead of doing the real thing.

On Friday the thirteenth, the weather has changed for the worse, and in line with this deterioration the battalion is on its way. The Manchesters arrive, looking terrible: most are new faces, but each face is shattered. They do not talk about who has been lost. Prior joins the battalion and we meet Colonel Marshall-of-the-Ten-Wounds, a bold, brave, but possibly reckless officer. Nerves are fraught, and in the night Hallet thinks he hears the roar of the guns when, in fact, it is simply the rocking horse in an upstairs room being moved by the wind coming through an open window.

Ten

We are in Melanesia again, as Rivers continues to reflect on the society and culture he investigated and left behind. He recalls seeing Ngea, one of the strongest men on the island, dying of a mysterious disease. He talked with Hocart about Njiru and the island, but soon after supper retired for the night. Rivers was disturbed by Mali, a girl of 13, crying as she lost her virginity to three men. Hocart and Rivers listened, and commented on how the culture was changing: the men were no longer head-hunters, were no longer treated as warriors by their women, and so they sat about talking, like 'old women'. Rivers and Hocart fell asleep and when they woke Rivers knew that Ngea had died. When they went to his hut they found the corpse bound and sitting upright. Njiru was ceremonially destroying the dead man's possessions as the women wailed. Ngea's body was taken to the beach and placed in an *era* — a stone enclosure. The next day Rivers went to Ngea's hut and found Ngea's wife Emele sitting in the same position as her dead husband; other women were outside, keeping a sort of vigil. At this point Njiru entered.

Rivers recalls a time when he, Hocart and Njiru visited the cave at Pa Na Keru. It was a sacred place, and was believed to be filled with ghosts. They moved into the inner cave, disturbing some bats, and he crouched in terror as they flew about him, eventually flying outwards, scaring the other men who accompanied them. Rivers and Njiru were alone, the one gripping the other, and when Rivers looked around he found that it was only the baby bats left hanging on the walls, waiting for the return of their mothers.

In his bed back in London, Rivers moves in and out of consciousness, the dark reminding him of the cave. Outside the cave Rivers reflected on what had happened, and believed that the most important experience that had taken place in the dark amid the flying bats was a sense of 'pure naked self-assertion. The right to be and to be *as one is*'. Njiru pointed out that a conch being sounded meant that the villagers had had a successful raid on a neighbouring enemy stronghold, and that only by taking a head — against the laws laid down by the British — would they ensure that any captives would be released.

Eleven

Billy Prior is describing the conditions in which the men have to live. It forces him to think about Rivers and the various theories he has put forth to Prior about the nature of conflict. Prior describes how the officers and men play football together — the 'only informal contact there is outside the line'. Prior notices that the expressions on the men's faces are changing, moving into 'a sort of *morose disgust*', and it is exclusively a face seen in the trenches.

Prior begins to notice the vulnerability of his men. The link, for him, between sex and death becomes increasingly pronounced as he stares at naked men waiting to shower. He reflects on his past as well, of the times spent at home on a Sunday, smelling his mother's cooking, reading a newspaper, singing hymns. There is an ominous atmosphere, as if something 'perfectly dreadful' is about to happen. The landscape is ruined. The men occupy themselves by preparing for a gas attack, and the only thing that raises morale is pay day. The bombardments increase in intensity, and the soldiers are moving in one direction: towards the Front.

Twelve

Rivers is still hallucinating: he imagines at one point that he is back in Ngea's hut, and that his sister, Kath, is sitting at the edge of his bed. He soon slips back into dreaming about Melanesia where he and Hocart were discussing whether the villagers would decapitate anyone and illegally revive head-hunting. Rivers decides to go to see

Namboko Taru (the woman Njiru treated for constipation) the next morning to discuss love charms. Several women were there, and they began to paint Rivers's face and flirt with him. He could find out little about Emele, stuck in the hut imitating her husband's posture, and became increasingly obsessed with her.

The heat continued to increase, to an intolerable pitch. Suddenly one day the conch sounded again and the villagers rushed to the beach to see a canoe coming to shore. Njiru walked out and took the bundle from Lembu. It was a four-year-old boy. The crowd that had gathered started celebrating and they returned to the village to see Emele come out of the hut for the first time since Ngea's death. Everyone was happy, except for the little boy, who looked on in fear and wonder.

Thirteen

Prior's battalion has advanced into German territory. They have broken through the Hindenburg Line and hopes are raised of a victory, although they are still under fire. Another battalion moves ahead of them, and with each footstep he takes Prior thinks the war is coming to a close.

But despair is not far away. He hears a 'guttural gurgling like a blocked drain' in No Man's Land and decides to investigate. It is Hallet. His brain is exposed, and one eye has gone; there is a hole where his left cheek used to be. Prior and Lucas try to drag him out using a rope, expecting him to die at any time, hoping he will die in fact, but he does not. In the evening the battalion pulls back, and it is at this point — either through exhaustion or because he has lost track of time — that Prior sees the setting sun rise. It disturbs him greatly.

Prior begins to reflect on the dead. Many of those he has been close to, including Longstaffe, have either been killed or are wounded. This section ends with him and Owen checking through the mail, two of Craiglockhart's 'success stories', but, as Prior sees them, 'objects of horror', who are, despite everything, at least still alive.

Part three

Fourteen

Rivers is reading the newspaper and notices that Prior would have been involved in the latest bloody conflict. Although well enough to eat breakfast, he is still ill.

Ngea's skull was bleached white by the sun. The little boy who had been taken by Lembu was, weeks after being taken, still dazed by the change in cultures. A ceremony was being prepared for placing Ngea's skull in the skull houses: pigs were slaughtered and cooked in celebration of the event. The skull was dressed in shells and creepers. Njiru raised the skull up to hush the crowd and prayed to the ghosts, offering them the sacrificial pig. Rivers noticed that this was a denuded culture, a people dying because of an absence of war: the birth rate was declining as their lives lost meaning and drive.

But some ceremonies survived. Rivers and Hocart witnessed a meeting between some villagers and the old ghosts who would visit to take the new ghost away. This was organised by Kundaite in Ngea's hut, and without Njiru's knowledge. After some silence they heard canoes approaching, and then a whistling sound, whose source Rivers could not locate, began. The 'ghosts' spoke to the natives and said that Ngea was in the room, and his wife, present with other women, began to wail. She was reassured by Kundaite that his soul was going to Sonto, and a better place.

When Hocart and Rivers returned to their tents they discussed what they had seen, and they noted that Njiru was not present at the ceremony. They were surprised to find an axe on Rivers's pillow, which belonged to Ngea. Rivers took this as a warning to stop asking so many awkward questions.

Fifteen

Prior remarks in his journal that Owen has put up a picture of Sassoon in his room, and it makes him think of being in Rivers's room at Craiglockhart. Prior's view of the hospital has changed: he no longer sees his being there as a sign of failure. Prior's bravery in getting Hallet out of No Man's Land has earned him a recommendation for the Military Cross, although he still does not know if rescuing Hallet, which meant that he would live, was the right thing to do.

The war is drawing to a close: the Austro-Hungarian Empire has collapsed, and there is talk of peace, but others are more sceptical, including Prior. The experienced soldiers, who cough repeatedly because of a recent gas attack, are joined by new, fresh-faced recruits from England, and they studiously avoid each other.

Prior continues to administer to the everyday realities of war: handing out parcels that have come from home and filling in forms. He thinks about a middle-aged man he bayoneted recently, and he is filled with regret. But life continues, and the battalion is entertained by a musical group called The Peddlers. When a particularly sentimental song is sung Prior is envious of those who have the emotional depths left to weep to it. The chapter ends with Prior writing that they return to the Front on 18 October.

Sixteen

Wansbeck and Rivers are talking on the ward; Wansbeck says that although the vision of the German soldier still haunts him almost every night, the imaginary smell has now 'gone', and Rivers takes this as a good sign. Wansbeck admits to not believing in an afterlife: he claims that he lost his faith when he saw the unburied corpses lying in No Man's Land. Both men talk about how such a vision can become manifest, and to some extent they agree that it is a projection of Wansbeck's guilt. The conversation makes Rivers think of another patient at Craiglockhart — Harrington — who also suffered from terrible hallucinations. Through analysis Harrington had managed to confront the sense of guilt he had over surviving the war when his best friend had died.

It is at this point that he sees a 'skull', but this is not Melanesia, instead this is Hallet, returned from the Front. His injuries are terrible, and he has been unable to speak since he was shot. Rivers is shocked by what he sees, and as he listens to the English rain he is transported, once again, to Melanesia, and to a time of apparently endless, torrential rain.

Once the rain had stopped he and Njiru visited a skull house, which was being rebuilt. On the way Rivers contemplated the nature of power, and what it meant to have knowledge, and he concluded that to have the former you must be able to use the latter. They reached the skull house and Njiru began the prayer of purification. Njiru went on to explain that in the past captives were kept alive, in expectation of their heads being needed. Then he took a skull and held it out for Rivers to take, a great honour. Rivers was aware that as a scientist he held this receptacle in something close to awe, and he realised that so too did Njiru, but for different reasons: Rivers saw it as the container of self-reflection whereas Njiru believed that it contained the spirit, the *tomate*.

Looking at Hallet he notices that he is in the 2nd Manchesters and he wonders if he knows Prior, and if so, whether he is capable of remembering him.

Seventeen

Prior writes in his journal that the landscape is one of 'utter devastation'; it is a poisoned land and, linking with the previous chapter, he notes that in 50 years' time farmers will continue to turn up skulls in these fields. He notes that death has desensitised the men, and that no sooner is somebody dead than they begin to fade from memory. The British are advancing quickly, moving through deserted trenches, apprehensive about the previously forbidden places they are visiting.

They continue to march, and it is Prior's job to round up the stragglers, bullying them into keeping up. He is just about to shout at one man when he notices that he is asthmatic. Prior takes pity on him and gets him into a horse ambulance. After a draining march they find themselves in what passes as a 'normal' landscape: farmland, cats, dogs and even women. As he writes his journal at a kitchen table Prior notes with some irony that only a few days ago a German soldier would have sat in the same place, looking at the same view.

After stopping for several days they march on, through a recently bombed village, and they know the enemy is close. One of the men, Wyatt, visits a prostitute and her daughters; Owen, who is homosexual, attracts unwelcome comments from the other men because he is so popular with local girls. Prior notices a young man in a farmyard watching him; he decides to follow him, and arranges to meet him later on that day. He gives the youth some cigarettes and they have sex in a country lane, with Prior commenting that where he has been no doubt many German officers have also been quite recently. The young man seems to encapsulate France: exploited and abused by first Germany and then Great Britain.

As the troops march, rumours begin to grow that Austria has signed a peace treaty, but there is no respite for Prior and his men: they will have to fight to the bitter end, 'sacrificed to the subclauses and the small print'.

The 2nd Manchesters reach an impasse: stuck in the line of fire beneath a German stronghold, unable to patrol except by night, and cut off from advancing by a canal. The fields surrounding the canal have been flooded by the retreating Germans in order to slow down the advance. The objective of the British attack — La Motte Farm — is uphill and surrounded by German machine guns. The choices are limited but, Prior notes dryly, they amount to creating either a mini-Passchendaele or a mini-Somme. Either way it is almost inevitable slaughter. The chances of success are zero. Prior writes one last letter to Rivers asking him to see his mother if he dies.

The tension begins to build as they wait for the order to attack. In that time Prior has to shoot a puppy because of the noise it makes, and it is done with a cruel casualness. As he waits, in a crowded room full of his colleagues, Prior thinks back to when he turned down Manning's offer of a desk job in London, and he has no regrets.

Eighteen

Rivers is in the hospital, attending to the everyday concerns of his patients. At the same time we are aware of Prior and Owen waiting for one of the last attacks of the war. Rivers has to inspect Hallet again, and he sees his family: a young brother, the retired military father, the exhausted mother and his fiancée. The family is moved out for Rivers to inspect the injured man, and as he looks at him Hallet's voice rises as a whisper, close to death, *mate*, as Njiru might have said. Rivers goes down the corridor to meet the family, passing the mother on the way back to her son. The father, although trying to keep his emotions under control, is clearly moved, proud of his son for being so 'bloody brave'. They all move back to the ward to see his last hours. Hallet is trying to say something: it sounds like 'Shotvarfet'. The family puts on a brave face, but the voice does not fade.

Rivers thinks of his last evening on the island. He recalls his last conversation with Njiru: they talked of spirits, and of the power of exorcism. Njiru was proud that one day he would feature in Rivers's book, but it was a book that was never written, another casualty of the war. Rivers's thoughts are disturbed by a noise from behind Hallet's screen: his voice is getting louder and the other patients are beginning to get irritated.

Meanwhile, back in France, Prior and his men are preparing to attack. At 5.45 a.m. hell erupts as they go over the top, to be met with a barrage of machine gun fire. Prior is running towards the enemy lines, shells whizzing overhead; he notices the engineers desperately trying to construct a bridge over the canal. He is almost immediately hit, and numbness, rather than pain, spreads over him. He sees Owen die, shot down mercilessly, and then he looks at himself in the water, and his vision fades as he dies.

'*Shotvarfet. Shotvarfet*'. Hallet's voice gets louder and louder and Rivers finally realises he is trying to say 'it's not worth it', and he tells Hallet's family. Other patients shout out their approval, and Major Hallet, desperately fighting his emotions, insists that the sacrifices are worth it. Hallet dies, his statement made, his naivety dead with him.

The attempt by the 2nd Manchesters to build a bridge over the canal in the last week of the war has failed. So many lives have been lost to something so futile. As Rivers slumps in his ward he sees Njiru coming down the corridor of the Empire Hospital, and he stares at Rivers, after declaring the end of life, of other empires, of other worlds.

Characters

Barker seldom describes her characters' physical appearance because she 'likes to let the reader decide how people are going to look'. She has also commented that: 'I think of my characters as normal people under immense pressure rather than as sufferers from mental illness. Why the immense pressure? Because you need to crack the shell to find out what's inside it.'

All three books in the *Regeneration* trilogy combine historical figures, such as Siegfried Sassoon, William Rivers and Wilfred Owen, with fictional characters, such as Billy Prior. The central, unifying character in all three novels is William Rivers. Rivers was a renowned anthropologist and psychiatrist who worked with shell-shocked patients at Craiglockhart Hospital near Edinburgh during and after the First World War. Famously, Rivers was the doctor who treated the poet Siegfried Sassoon in 1917.

Captain William Rivers

> Rivers is one of the real characters…he was a psychiatrist who joined the army in 1915, as soon as he could. He was an anthropologist before the war, but he had a medical degree, so he went back to practising medicine for the duration of the war. And he was a very humane, a very compassionate person who was tormented really by the suffering he saw, and very sceptical about the war, but at the same time he didn't feel he could go the whole way and say no, stop.

> 'A backdoor into the present: an interview with Pat Barker' by Wera Reusch

William Halse Rivers (1864–1922) was a psychologist and anthropologist. He was born in Chatham in Kent, the eldest brother to two sisters and a brother. The family held that William was named after the midshipman who shot the sniper who killed Lord Nelson, and this is alluded to in The Ghost Road. Rivers went to Tonbridge School, and then to the University of London. He left to join St Bartholomew's Hospital in London and became the youngest medical graduate in the hospital's history when he gained an MB and then an MRCS in 1886. He was not content to remain a hospital doctor though, and he often undertook sea voyages in the late 1880s as a ship's surgeon. He also researched neurological experiments with Victor Horsley. As in the novel, in real life Rivers had a pronounced stammer.

In 1892 he travelled to Jena and it was here that he became convinced that he wanted to work in the relatively new area of psychoanalysis. When he returned to England he took up a post at the Bethlem Royal Hospital. He also lectured on experimental psychology at University College Hospital. In 1893 Rivers was teaching psychology at Cambridge; in 1902 he was elected a fellow of St John's College; and in 1907 he was made director of Cambridge University's new psychology laboratory.

In 1898 Rivers travelled to the Torres Strait where he developed his interest in anthropological studies; he spent time in southwest India in 1901–02. In 1907 he travelled to the Solomon Islands, as well as other islands in Melanesia and Polynesia, and it is these excursions that form the basis of Barker's descriptions in *The Ghost Road*.

During this time Rivers continued to read the work of Carl Jung and Sigmund Freud, and in 1915 he took this knowledge with him to the Maghull Military Hospital where he worked as a physician. In October 1916 he was sent to Craiglockhart Hospital for Officers just outside Edinburgh. Here he pioneered new techniques in dealing with shell-shocked soldiers through psychoanalysis. In 1917 he was posted to the Royal Flying Corps Central Hospital in Hampstead where he continued with this work. After the war he drew on his experiences as a psychoanalyst and anthropologist to write on subjects as diverse as the nature of instinct and the importance of dreams. He was a socialist who supported the Labour Party, and he was even selected as one of its candidates in the General Election of 1922, but he died before any votes were cast. He was unmarried.

As in real life, Rivers uses psychoanalysis to treat his patients in Barker's novels. He was passionate about his work, which he saw as a vocation. But, throughout the *Regeneration* trilogy, he is acutely aware of the tragic **paradox** that he is curing his patients only to send them back to fight and possibly die. This morally conflicted position eats away at him throughout the novel. How can he accept his relationship with his patients if it is based on this obvious treachery? In life and in *The Ghost Road* he sought a humane cure that attempted to understand the cause of trauma, and to treat it through exploring its origins. In other words, he wanted to unearth the nature of repression, using techniques that are recognisably Freudian. He has also been traumatised by an event that remains largely mysterious to the reader and that robbed him of a visual memory. The real-life Rivers was an almost stereotypically repressed Englishman: homosexual (at a time when it was illegal) and shy. Dealing with men — such as Sassoon — who shared the same sexuality but who had to keep it concealed (to varying degrees) must have tested Rivers's cool objectivity a great deal.

Rivers's relationship with his patients is not what we would expect of his rank (captain) and status (doctor). The beginning of chapter two is in stark contrast to chapter one: the visceral sexuality of Billy Prior is contrasted with the sublimated sexuality characterised by the 'crude copies' of Tenniel's drawings from *Alice in Wonderland*. Rivers's link with Dodgson is expanded upon. This develops the theme of repressed sexuality with Rivers describing to a patient, Elliot Smith, his relationship with Charles Dodgson (aka Lewis Carroll). Rivers's identity is established by Barker, but it is interesting to note how close to Rivers's own voice this depiction is. This is not a sympathetic self-portrait; indeed, to some extent it explains Rivers's uncertainty about himself because we view him as a flawed, vulnerable character.

Rivers's treatment of Moffet extends still further the ambiguous nature of sexuality in this novel. The patient is 'defiant, nervous, full of fragile, ungrounded pride', and he has been unable to walk for three months. Rivers believes that the problem is psychological, that the inability to walk is due to hysterical paralysis, and he aims to cure it in an unconventional way: by drawing stocking tops on his legs. The language is charged with sexual innuendo and literary allusion: Moffet is compared to 'a supercilious rabbit', linking again to *Alice*, and he says to Rivers that '"gradually, day by day, you propose to...um...*lower* the stockings, and as the stockings are *unrolled*, so to speak, the...er...paralysis will..." A positive orgy of twitching. "Retreat."' Here we see how Rivers's thought patterns move from subject to subject, making connections between the private and public (Katharine, his sister who was adored by Dodgson, is also, he suspects, suffering from the same condition as Moffet).

Over the course of the novel Rivers evolves from being simply a sounding board for other characters' thoughts and emotions into a rounded character capable of exploring and analysing his own flawed personality. His recent and more distant pasts are assembled before us to show us how much we are products of conscious and unconscious actions; the present acts as a lens on the past. A chance comment by his sister Kath forces him to think about what he has repressed in his life, an image that has haunted him and made him almost completely delete his visual memory. The past is there to be made sense of, to make a pattern of, to establish a narrative from, but it is also rendered as a series of unrelated or chance encounters that only gain meaning through retrospection.

This is the final volume of the *Regeneration* trilogy and Barker allows Rivers, to some extent, to regenerate himself: he exorcises some of his ghosts through revisiting his time in Melanesia, and in doing so he is better able to understand himself. However, we do not see him completely reconciled with himself: the novel ends ambiguously with Njiru approaching a possibly still-delusional Rivers on the ward of his hospital, suggesting that the past is increasingly active in his conscious self, questioning him and judging him. Furthermore, the strong undercurrents of the text (most obviously his suggested homosexuality) have not been confronted in any real and lasting sense. The past has an uncomfortable relationship with the present, but this is a truer reflection of life than a satisfactorily neat conclusion. Rivers, although more fulfilled at the end of novel than at the beginning, is not fully regenerated; indeed, the ongoing casualties being sent back to England — culminating in Hallet's death — remind him of the invidious position he has found himself in: namely, that he is a doctor who is charged with making men well enough to return to fight and possibly die.

Lieutenant Billy Prior

Billy Prior is, according to one critic, 'the trilogy's most memorable creation: a sexually violent, keenly intelligent, and very disturbing man whose mind games with Rivers causes the psychiatrist to question himself, his motivation, and his morality' (Mariella Frostrup, *Open Book*). He is a working-class officer from the north of England. In *Regeneration* he is a patient of Rivers's at Craiglockhart War Hospital. He has been traumatised by the death of two friends and is suffering from mutism and severe asthma. He has been sent back from the Front several times in the war, but is always anxious to return. At the end of *Regeneration* the Board recommends that he is not returned to combat because of his asthma; the decision causes him to have a breakdown because, he feels, he will not be able to prove himself as a soldier.

Barker does not describe her characters' physical appearances in any detail, but Prior is thin, tough, 'a little, spitting, sharp-boned alley cat' with a northern accent, 'not ungrammatical, but with the vowel sounds distinctly flattened'. Rivers thinks he has 'great powers of detachment' which, according to Prior, can be translated as him being a 'cold-blooded little bastard'. He later notices that his eyes are 'trustless'.

His parents are difficult, and their relationship with their son — as we see through small, skilfully handled glimpses in *The Ghost Road* — is not easy. His father thinks he was a fool to fight ('I told him, time enough to do summat for the Empire when the Empire's done summat for you,' he says on p. 56 of *Regeneration*) and, unlike Rivers, his father believes that his going to the Front has nothing to do with idealism and everything to do with pragmatism: he simply wanted to escape being a shipping clerk. Worse, perhaps, he has become engaged to a girl who is below him in social rank, and his homosexuality has become known (at least to his family).

He is a deeply divided character, and his sexuality is one manifestation of this almost schizoid approach to life, but there are others: he has a complicated notion of duty, preferring to fight for a country he seems to have become alienated from rather than stay safely at home. There is, as in other war literature, a sense of responsibility to the men, rather than to the 'cause' itself, and this helps explain why, at the beginning of the novel, Prior is so determined to be sent back to the Front.

He wrestles with many conflicts: not only is he bisexual (and seemingly voracious in his appetites) but he is also reckless, with both men and women, choosing anyone from a superior officer to a street-walking prostitute. He is an articulate mute, an officer who is familiar with the underclass, a working-class lad from the North who spends much of his time in the company of public-school educated gentlemen from the South. He crosses many borders, but it could be argued that his natural home, in a psychological sense, is No Man's Land.

His journey is one from peace to conflict, but in the course of that journey he, more than Rivers, comes to a point of peace before the final assault at the end of the novel: he reflects on the choices he has made and does not regret them. That is not to say that his death — and that of those about him — is not judged harshly by Barker, but we sense that Prior, unlike the other characters in the novel, has a command of his fate: he chooses to go back to the Front, just as he chooses to have sex at certain times, and with certain characters. At no point in the novel do we feel that he is dictated to by others, nor do we believe that his life is compromised by the choices he has made. He dies, ultimately, in a futile action, just as Owen did, and both men symbolise the lost generation who were sacrificed by four dying empires. Prior, with his more meritocratic and liberated view of life, symbolises a future generation waiting to be born from the rubble of the Great War. That he is so complex and troubled a character suggests that a new world order will be anything but at ease with itself, especially as it comes to terms with the scale of its loss.

Other characters

Billy Prior and William Rivers dominate the book, but it would be a mistake to assume that a character lacks depth and complexity simply because he or she does not occupy many pages in the text. Take, for example, Elinor, the red-haired prostitute that Prior has sex with at the beginning of chapter three. She is a memorable character in many ways: strong, yet vulnerable at the same time, symbolic of a certain class of woman (she reminds him of another prostitute from his past — Lizzie — who also does 'her bit' for the war effort), but clearly defined in her own right. The exchanges she has with Prior — both physical and verbal — are among the most powerful in the novel.

The same can be said of Hallet: here is a young man filled with an ardent belief in the war effort (see p. 144 for example), but who, over the course of only a few pages, personifies in many ways the movement from idealism to realism, from hope to despair, from life to death. It is he who ends the novel, inarticulately claiming that the war is 'not worth it', giving voice, as only the injured can, to the hollowness of his sacrifice.

The characters in the passages set in Melanesia are no less vivid: Njiru, the 'deformed' spiritual leader of the tribe, has authority. He is described as 'remarkable' with eyes that were 'hooded, piercing, intelligent, shrewd. Wary' (p. 127). Njiru is seen as the mirror image of Rivers: an authority in his own field, a man interested in what lies below the surface. To some extent he remains mysterious because we view much of these episodes from Rivers's perspective, and much of what *he* sees is open to speculation, but beyond comprehension. Melanesia remains enigmatic, as indeed do many of the characters who fill that stage.

The novel itself is remarkable for many reasons, but the characters who act as a supporting cast are skilfully developed: Major Telford, Ada, Kath, Hocart, Manning, and of course Wilfred Owen, each provide us with insights into how the human condition is affected by extreme conditions. That Prior and Rivers are so memorable should not blind us to the fact that without the minor characters the novel would be significantly less powerful: much of its psychological reach comes from the accomplished characterisation.

The psychology of war

In an interview Pat Barker said that: '…one of the things that impresses me is that two things happen to soldiers in war: a) they get killed or b) they come back more or less alright. It's really focussing on the people who do come back but don't come back alright, they are either physically disabled or mentally traumatised.'

Billy Prior is traumatised by the war: in the first book of the trilogy — *Regeneration* — he suffers from mutism, a psychological disorder induced by witnessing the death of two close friends at the Front. He is able to communicate with Rivers, at first, only through writing. Prior eventually finds his voice again after being treated by Rivers, but Barker is careful to make clear that trauma can be found at home as well as at the Front, and the one can be as scarring as the other. Prior escaped to the trenches because, like many men, it was better than life at home; his father bullied him and in *Regeneration* he claims that 'there was only one time I put my oar in' and that was when he hit Billy in the face 'to toughen 'em up'. Such typical 'masculine' conditioning is constantly subverted by Barker through the behaviour of Prior: his aggression, his bisexuality, his desire to reject his homeland, his sensitivity; all these factors are seen to be reactions to his unhappy upbringing. The war, although it does undoubtedly exacerbate Prior's feelings of alienation, is not its sole cause; indeed, in many ways Prior, like Sassoon, feels that he belongs to his men more than he does to his country, and this heightened sense of loyalty to one's regiment is actively promoted by the British Army and is seen as the bedrock for its success in many conflicts. Ironically, Prior, like others in the *Regeneration* trilogy, is a good soldier because he chooses his regiment over his family.

Rivers, in his own very different way, has been traumatised by his upbringing. The view of conflict that he witnessed — in a picture at the top of his stairs — has also impaired his ability to communicate fluently and to sustain a visual memory (p. 95). And just as trauma makes Prior a good soldier, so too it makes Rivers a good psychologist. Trauma, then, is presented by Barker as a way of explaining and exploring character and behaviour; although, as the last pages show, it is not romanticised. Hallet's final words — of the war not being worth it — and the noises of approval they received from others on the ward, confirm that for those denied a voice, and another chance of life lived through the experience that shapes them, the war is brutal and unfair.

Barker's message seems to be that there is no such thing as cultural supremacy: the societies that Rivers and his group of anthropologists explore before the war, although outwardly primitive, are not inferior to a European culture that will introduce killing on an industrial scale. The political and cultural imperialism that the West imposes on the Polynesians emasculates the villagers: the men become lesser versions of themselves because they are denied their traditional roles. Ironically, the desire to hunt, kill and to head-hunt is linked closely to the survival of the tribes; denied these deeply inherited norms of behaviour they lose the motive to live and procreate. So 'what they lived for' is denied them: they are now a 'people perished from the absence of war'. There is an undisguised irony here: as we move between West and East, masculine and feminine, past and present, Prior and Rivers, we are constantly reminded that whereas the Polynesians are literally dying from peace, the Europeans are dying from war: the battlefronts in this book are culturally and psychologically — rather than geographically and politically — defined. Man is broken by the unnatural, and so for the West to force itself on another culture will inevitably mean breakdown. Equally, for soldiers to be forced into new and artificial behaviour will result in their disintegration. Prior comments approvingly on Rivers's theory that 'the crucial factor in accounting for the vast number of breakdowns this war has produced is not the horrors…but the fact that the strain has to be borne in conditions of immobility, passivity and helplessness'. In other words, trauma occurs when something that is unnatural is imposed on a victim, and this occurs collectively and individually in *The Ghost Road*.

The nature of Prior's death is bleak because it seems to be so devoid of meaning. The slaughter of the Manchesters as they attempt to build a bridge is deeply upsetting for several reasons. First, we know that this was one of the last major offensives in a war that was, by then, effectively finished, and so the outcome of this battle had no bearing on the German surrender. Second, this was the incident in which one of the war's most powerful voices — Wilfred Owen — died, and that alone is seen as a terrible waste of genius. Third, the bridge itself seems almost a symbol of the need to make contact with the other side and failing at the very outset. Death is seen as 'banal, simple, repetitive' by Prior: there is nothing profound in his mind as he dies, no inner peace, no greater sense of what life means. At the end of this troubled — but independent — existence all he can conclude is that it is a 'balls up. Bloody mad'. This sense of madness runs through the book: Rivers tries to render such a term more explicable, but there is little one can do to make collective actions of mass destruction more palatable to those who are affected by it. The young Hallet's final condemnation of his father and the insanity that he, as a commanding officer, personifies, offers some glimmer of hope that the younger generation may conceivably see that such sacrifices are not worth it. The reality is that 20 years later such bloodshed would be seen again.

Themes

Sex and class

The breakdown of the old social order is not viewed negatively by Barker: indeed, there is a glimpse of a new, less rigid order beginning in chapter nine: here, Owen, Prior, Hallet and Potts — all officer class but all from slightly different social classes — live in a solidly bourgeois house in a suburban street. It seems a vision, albeit one bent out of shape by the war and by their circumstances, of what is to come: these are the homes of 'men making their way in the world', a new meritocracy perhaps. By living side by side these men are returned to something human: they cook, swim and laugh, and indeed at one point Barker writes that 'somewhere on the Somme he had mislaid the capacity to be surprised, but the next few days were a constant succession of surprises' (p. 142). With the breakdown in certainties come new experiences and new insights, and they are nowhere more clearly seen than here. Of course, it cannot last: the war grinds on, and even the house that they live in, solid though it is, is 'bleeding quietly from its unstaunchable wound' (p. 145).

The old order is changing, and to some extent the passages set in Melanesia remind us of this: the British Empire has peaked, and the casual exploitation of other cultures will no longer be tolerated. The world of Rivers represents a world that, in its acceptance of cultural relativism and Freudian psychoanalysis, places ever greater emphasis on the individual rather than the group, on autonomy rather than an empire. The final betrayal at the end of the novel is telling: Hallet exposes the lie of his father, and in doing so shows how the system — ruined and inherently corrupt — had begun to reach its endgame in 1918.

Prior breaks established class taboos in the novel. He is a working-class northerner who becomes an officer, but he never loses an awareness of the class divisions that run throughout society in general and the British Army in particular. To some extent he exploits the idiosyncrasies to his own end: he dominates Charles, both emotionally and sexually, and it is a relationship that is based on an inverted sadomasochistic exploitation of the upper-class Manning by the working-class Prior. Prior does not conceal his disgust for those — like Birtwhistle — who have nothing but contempt for the working class. Birtwhistle, a Cambridge don, refers to his working-class lover as his WC, a conscious connection with a water closet or toilet. Barker is keen to explore this highly charged area, and she admits that she does it through Prior:

> I found Prior a delight to write about!…and his sexuality is part of this. There was certainly in England at that time a sense among the upper classes that sex was something you did with the lower classes because it belongs to the animal side of your own nature. And Prior is very aware of this and plays on it and plays up to it. But at the same time he very deeply despises it, he refers to working class youths and for a certain kind of man they are a seminal-spittoon.

To some extent Prior represents a figure out of a D. H. Lawrence novel: northern and working class, enigmatic and an iconoclast, sexually promiscuous, provocative, impulsive and arrogant. He is, in many ways, a man of his time. Prior's contact with Birtwhistle makes him feel contaminated: he is suspicious of relationships that are exploitative of his class and to some extent this explains why he favours being in the army. Here, officers and men can play together — 'street corner football played in the spirit of public-school rugby' — and this allows him to lose his identity, his former self. Prior moves between the classes but he, more than any other character in the novel, shows how social mobility, although often desirable, is fraught with difficulties for both the individual and those who seek to accommodate him. Prior is as uncomfortable with the working class as he is with the upper middle class, and the only thing that seems to allow him to attach himself to either is sex, and this is invariably only done on his own, predatory, terms. If Prior is the **personification** of a less rigid social hierarchy then it is clear that it is no less problematic than that which, owing to the war, has been swept away.

Sex and relationships

Sex is rarely linked with love in this novel. Men seem to seek out any means of sexual relief, and they do so, very often, in a utilitarian, functional way. Prior's sexual inter-course with Nellie the prostitute (pp. 37–43) is sordidly unpleasant: there is nothing approaching love, or even lust, here. Barker writes that Prior 'groped around in his mind for the appropriate feeling of disgust, and found excitement instead, no, more than that, the sober certainty of power' (p. 40). The encounter sends Prior back to his own past, to when he charged his teacher — Father Mackenzie — for sex, and this in turn forces him to project his own self-disgust on to her because 'the only way not to be her was to hate her'. The episode is linked with exploitation and death; it even concludes with Prior smelling gas, a powerful reminder of the trenches. Prior's first attempt to have sex with his fiancée, Sarah, took place on a gravestone 'which in retrospect seems a rather appropriate start for a relationship so hedged by death' he writes.

There are occasional displays of attraction and affection, but even these are sometimes likened to animalistic behaviour (for example, an officer crossing his legs to attract the attention of interested men is compared to 'a baboon's bottom' on p. 103). Sex seems to be another form of control, and so when Prior cannot publicly argue with Birtwhistle for his offensive remarks on the working class he decides to exact his revenge in the bedroom: 'nothing like *sexual* humiliation...Nobody ever forgets that,' he says to Rivers on p. 100. Other, more minor, characters have a similar, brutalised experience of sex: Brennan started out as a 'blackbirder' (p. 123), a trader who kidnaps natives and tries to have sex with the females. For him women of any race can be traded for sex.

It seems little different in Melanesia. Rivers's work reveals how sex is paid for by the man to the girl's parents, and in a moment of male and cultural bonding Rinambesi, Njiru and Rivers laugh aloud at how many women Rinambesi has 'had fuck-fuck' with. The exploitation of women for sex is catalogued elsewhere as Mali, a girl of 13, is raped by three men (p. 157). There is only the routine grind of sex, with no love, and little or no hope of children (p. 158).

There is also a clear link between sex and death: after having sex with Sarah Prior flings 'the rubber into the fire, a million or so Billies and Sarahs perishing in a gasp of flame'. Later, he writes in his journal: 'I told Rivers once that the sensation of going over the top was sexy...there *was* something in common — racing blood, risk, physical exposure, a kind of awful daring about it.' In Melanesia *mate*, which is of course the English verb for procreation, is defined 'in all the dictionaries' as dead; and on another island — Eddystone — 'ghosts and sex *did* go together'. Perhaps tellingly the only sexual relationship that seems genuinely passionate is that of Jenkins and his wife, a character we never meet but whose letters are so intense that they make Prior feel ashamed. His letter to Sarah, in contrast, will not trouble any censor.

Elsewhere in the novel sex can be used as a **metaphor** for war itself: when Prior and his men take over a French village, shortly after the German Army has vacated it, he has sex with a young man who, almost certainly, has traded his body for a packet of German cigarettes very recently. The young man's body, it seems, is France itself: abused, exploited, traded and disregarded by first the Germans and then the British. Only when they have both left will it be able to find its own identity.

Innocence and experience

The passages relating to Charles Dodgson (the real name of Lewis Carroll, the Cambridge mathematician and author of *Alice's Adventures in Wonderland*) are among the most interesting and unusual in the novel. The movement between Rivers's past and present is rapid: the psychologist contemplates some crude copies of Tenniel's illustrations of *Alice* when he is on Ward Seven of a former children's hospital. The overt phallic symbolism of Alice's snake neck is described by Elliot Smith as 'interesting', a remark that starts Rivers thinking about his own childhood.

Snakes are central to these passages, although Barker, through Rivers, rather knowingly notes that 'evidently snakes had lost the right to be simply snakes', which warns against a psychoanalytical interpretation of something that, paradoxically, is open to many meanings.

Most obviously this is the moment in Rivers's development that marked the end of innocence and the beginning of experience: Dodgson's work is obsessed with the retention of (particularly female) innocence in the face of mysterious forces of adulthood; in Rivers's recollections of the elderly writer we are told of his fear of snakes — a commonly used phallic symbol in Freudian psychoanalysis — and his equal dislike of boys (who he describes as 'a mistake'). In this episode Rivers recalls that when he asks why boys are viewed by Dodgson as a mistake he is told that it is because they 'are rough and noisy. And they fight'. He realises that this view of masculinity, limited though it is, nevertheless defines what it means to be a man in the modern age. The portrayal of Dodgson is vivid and insightful: it marks the shaping of Rivers's reflective self, and in employing another real character who lived and wrote along the dangerous fault line of child and adult sexuality, Barker is able to explore the tensions that run through the developing mind.

Symbols — such as those portrayed in Tenniel's drawings — are ways of deciphering the complex; drawing a snake's body onto the body of a young girl, consciously or not, fuses innocence and experience, and their inevitable collision is a way to allow the reader to understand the subject's otherwise concealed complexity. The fact that this episode is interspersed with Rivers's treatment of a young man damaged by war further illustrates the conflict between innocence and experience, of which war is the most extreme example.

Hallet is seen as naive, a character who is almost fated to be destroyed by the grim reality of a cynical war. When he, Prior, Potts and Owen rest in a deserted house in the French countryside, they are aware of a 'fragile civilisation, a fellowship on the brink of disaster' (pp. 142–43). It is he who, when arguing with Potts about the war, says that the conflict was principally concerned with protecting the sovereignty of small nations (Potts describes him as a 'naive idiot'). Hallet is from a military family and a public school, and his self-assurance is that of the establishment, but his innocence is in sharp contrast to those of the other, experienced soldiers, and his claim that 'this is still a just war' marks him out as being 'like a little boy'.

Barker's purpose in including this character is obvious: he reminds us of the ardent optimism that propelled so many young men into the war at its outset. His existence is complex. Coming from a strong, officer-class background he would seem to be less vulnerable than the others; indeed, Barker writes that he has about him the 'illusion of fragility'. His understanding of the war seems entirely superficial. For instance, he cannot understand why a flypaper he has bought to kill wasps and other insects is thrown away by Prior because it reminds him of the flies on the dead of the Somme (and even his language of rebuke is childlike — he warns them not to 'blame *me* if you all get tummy upsets').

His death is the death not only of innocence, but also of a way of seeing war as a noble pursuit. His parents are **caricatures** of the upper-class English who suffered in so many ways from the war. Hallet had to die to show us how much the establishment had to lose. He, not Prior, has to scream that 'it's not worth it' at the end to show just how much innocence has been lost. His battle with the truth 'was every man's battle' (p. 269).

Identity and belonging

Identity is seen as blurred or moveable in much of Barker's fiction, and one area that interests her is 'border country' (see, for example, a later novel of hers entitled *Border Crossing*), or No Man's Land. Her fiction is constantly asking us to think about where we belong: is it in England, France or Melanesia? In peacetime or in times of conflict? In the past or the present? And how much of our identity is fixed, secure, or rooted in one place?

To some extent none of the characters in this novel belong to any one place. Rivers seems divided between Melanesia and England; Prior is divided between France and England; even the natives of Melanesia seem to be increasingly alienated from their homeland as it is changed by imperial powers from Europe. If setting is fundamental to our own identities then all the characters in this novel are displaced. The world has been turned upside down, and so what we should be fighting for — our homeland — has been replaced by something more tangible and personal. Prior belongs in a more transient, nomadic world where we are no longer defined by nationality, but instead by our actions and our dispositions, our sexuality and our class. It is an ambiguous existence, and one that can be seen to be close to a psychological 'No Man's Land'. Indeed, Prior's desire to go 'back to the Front' has several meanings in itself: it suggests a sexual dichotomy, or dilemma, for a bisexual man, but it also articulates the confused condition that soldiers were in at the time. Their places are dislodged, and what once was taken as a given — namely, that we are subjects willing to die for our country, and indeed celebrate the sacrifice — has also gone. If it is possible to belong in the trenches then Prior does, but this is not because the trenches are tolerable. It is, instead, that what once was seen as secure and honest has been destabilised by its own hypocrisy.

Fate and free will

When the four men are left alone Owen speculates that they might just conceivably have been forgotten by the British Army. 'Shut up!' Potts says to him and then Barker writes (p. 147):

> Everybody touched wood, crossed fingers, groped for lucky charms: all the small, protective devices of men who have no control over their own fate. No use, Prior thought. Somewhere, outside the range of human hearing, and yet heard by all of them, a clock had begun to tick.

If fate exists, it exists in the battle plans of the 'top brass', not with God or some divine power. Or it could be argued that character is fate: that Prior had to die because he was compelled to return to the Front to fight with his men. Equally, Rivers seems destined to become a psychiatrist and an anthropologist given his early experiences. But what does Barker seem to be saying? That there is no free will at all? That we are at the mercy of greater forces? To some extent, yes, but that does not mean that we do not have any freedom to act. The point is that there are forces at work that are more powerful than individuals. A metaphor for this occurs on p. 85: Prior and Sarah are saying goodbye to each other as they wait on the station platform. For a moment they are surprised and astonished by a flock of birds that swoops and turns against the sky. As they watch they are 'drunk on the sight of so much freedom, their linked hands slackening, able, finally, to think of nothing, as the train steamed in'. The train is fate, and the characters are powerless to escape it, but that does not mean they cannot look upon the momentary revelation of the free.

Although the passages set in Melanesia might ostensibly suggest that there is a more 'natural' and unfettered existence elsewhere, Barker makes it clear that the natives are just as restricted by exterior forces as those who die on the battlefields of France: the political decisions made by imperial powers decide the fate of those who live under that rule of law. But the fact is that character is fate as well, and Rivers's research shows us that we are all governed by impulses and actions that transcend culturally defined norms: 'any suppressed memory stores up trouble for the future', and this is as applicable to the people of Melanesia as it is to Prior. How they expel such suppressed emotions, and what system of belief they adopt to make sense of it, depends on many factors. However, ultimately, as Rivers remarks, above us is only an 'empty sky'.

Masculinity and femininity

Masculinity is challenged throughout the novel. The central character, Billy Prior, is a complex mix of characteristics, some of which could be loosely termed masculine, others possibly feminine. His ambiguous sexuality is at the heart of this often confusing picture: he is bisexual, but he never really seems to view sex as anything other than something purely functional. He can be aggressive and passive, highly sensitive and extremely brutal and blunt, self-doubting and very brave. Barker's aim is undoubtedly to make us question what it means to be a hero in the context of war. Strictly speaking, Prior is a criminal because homosexuality was illegal in England at the time, but the fact that it seems so common points out the hypocrisy of the country's establishment.

Central to a perception of masculinity is man's propensity to fight, and Barker subverts this view throughout *The Ghost Road*. It is a release, and as we have seen elsewhere, it rarely offers him anything other than transient relief.

Elsewhere in the novel masculinity is intrinsically linked to sexuality and violence. Major Telford, for example, believes that a nurse has castrated him and pickled his penis in formaldehyde: he is delusional, but his condition is indicative of a profound self-doubt expressed elsewhere in the novel: namely that men no longer know what is expected of them. The men on the Melanesian islands that Rivers visits can no longer head-hunt, and this loss is more than the denial of a ritual, it acts like another form of castration. They are denied something that characterised their role as men, and without it they become listless. Elsewhere, on p. 21 Moffet is treated for paralysis (which is imaginary) by having stocking tops drawn on his leg by Rivers, who then re-draws them every day, restoring feeling to the newly uncovered areas. The lines drawn on his skin, erased every day, seem to symbolise the faint and insubstantial boundaries between masculinity and femininity. Each is being redrawn in this conflict, either through psychoanalysis or by the nature of the conflict itself.

The female characters in *The Ghost Road* are not fully fleshed out. In fact, they are, like the male characters, defined through sex and class. The first woman we meet — Louie — is described, through Prior's eyes, as 'gloriously, devastatingly, *fuckably* common' (p. 5). Prior's fiancée, Sarah, although more developed than the other female characters, rarely becomes more than an appendage to Prior himself. The longest episode she appears in involves a hurried and seemingly loveless act of sexual intercourse. Elsewhere there are prostitutes (Lizzie and Nellie), nurses, several female natives (who are seen as either mothers or sex objects) and several mothers (who, if they are middle class, are usually passive figures, but if working class are more truculent and blunt). Nowhere in the novel do we really begin to understand why these women are attracted to these men, either as lovers or wives.

Religion

God seems absent from this novel; indeed, Rivers looks up 'at the blue, empty sky and realized that…No bearded elderly white man looked down on them' (pp. 119–20) Does this mean, as Rivers goes on to contemplate, that within this novel the 'whole frame of social and moral rules' collapses? What are the implications for society if we accept this view?

For Rivers the difference between an absent and present god is revealed to him on the island of Vao. There a child is ritually killed (p. 104), and he associates this with a memory taken from one of his father's churches. Here he recalls seeing a scene in a stained glass window depicting Abraham about to slay his son, and Barker writes that:

The two events represented the difference between savagery and civilization, for in the second scenario the voice of God is about to forbid the sacrifice, and will be heeded.

But in the societies that he works in, father figures — and, ultimately, deities — have abandoned their children to their fates. Now, in this absence, millions are sacrificed in a ritual slaughter that they have no understanding of, nor way of altering its path. The link between the ancient and modern cultures is clear: a divine being is absent, the sky empty. The gods that Njiru worships are unable to intervene to save lives or cultures, and in an increasingly rational, scientific world, traditions, myths and entire cultures will be gradually worn away. And the further we get from our natural state the closer we get to a hell, which is not just the Somme, but is also 'a deserted washroom at night, all white tiles and naked lights'. For Prior this 'is the most convincing portrayal of hell the human mind can devise' because it is clinical, clean, soulless, dead and essentially human.

For Prior — with his ironically religious name — religion is more closely bound up with exploitation, and this helps explain his dislike of it. His encounter with Nellie the prostitute induces a self-loathing that can be directly linked to his sexual encounters with his priest, Father Mackenzie, as a young boy. This is developed later on when he has to leave the meeting of evangelicals because, again, it reminds him of his past ('Father Mackenzie…What a teacher the man was — in or out of his cassock', p. 79). For Prior religion is akin to a death cult: 'We have to die, we don't have to worship it' he says to Sarah, and it is the voice of someone who has witnessed many unnecessary — and random — tragic acts. Death is a state of nothingness, and he contemplates this when he views a photograph of Sarah's first fiancé, Johnny, his face beginning to fade, which 'seemed almost to be an unintended symbol of the oblivion into which we all go'.

Symbols

A symbol is an object that represents something else (and it can represent many different things simultaneously). We use symbols all the time. Some would argue that life is so complex that it can only be understood through a series of symbols: think of a dove symbolising peace, a swastika symbolising Nazism, a poppy symbolising remembrance. Words themselves can be symbolic of ideas: 'peace' as a semantic unit symbolises the concept it spells out.

Snakes

The episode involving Charles Dodgson, Rivers's family, and various snakes, is a barely concealed study in phallic symbolism and the move from innocence to experience (Rivers once asked his father why the devil took the form of a snake, and the discarded snakeskin on p. 23 is suggestive of a used condom). It is here that there is one of the first mentions of a ghost, meaning a lost presence, a memory of what once existed. The link with sex is clear: Katharine, his sister, is said to have sat on an adder, and when the snake is tipped out onto a rug Dodgson and her father beat it to death in what seems to be a ritualistic killing of sexual knowledge. Rivers contemplates the meaning of such symbols and concludes that 'the task of making meaningful connections was quite unusually difficult. A good deal of innocence had been lost in recent years', meaning, perhaps, that not only has the war destroyed what innocence there was left in society, but that psychoanalysis had rendered an innocent reading of objects impossible: 'evidently snakes had lost the right to be simply snakes' Rivers says to himself. Such a comment is a direct reference to Freud's analysis of phallic symbols in *The Interpretation of Dreams*. In this landmark publication (first published in German in 1899) Freud argues that some everyday objects (which are capable of 'penetration') commonly experienced in dreams — for example: sticks, trees, swords — are derived from an understanding of the male sexual organ. Post-Freud, Rivers seems to be suggesting, otherwise innocent things have become loaded with meaning.

Ghosts

Not surprisingly references to ghosts appear regularly in this novel. They linger with the living, haunting their continued existence, reminding those who survive of the fragility of life, inducing guilt. Prior is aware of Johnny, Sarah's first fiancé, staring at him 'inanely' from a photograph in her bedroom. Both Prior and Rivers seem to have a heightened sense of ghosts: indeed, Prior admits to himself that there are 'Ghosts everywhere. Even the living were only ghosts in the making', and given the nature of war, of the profound transience of everything, even the present has a 'quality of *remembered* experience' (p. 46). We follow in the footsteps of others: Prior has sex with a prostitute, aware that he is lying in the sperm of a previous customer; he sleeps in the bed once slept in by Sarah's first fiancé; Rivers is named after William Rivers of the *Victory*; Mrs Irving — Rivers's landlady — keeps a portrait of her dead son over her mantelpiece 'with flowers beneath it and candlesticks on either side' (p. 116); Wilfred Owen is known as the Ghost (p. 180). Life itself seems to be the ghost of what it should be and such an idea is shared in Melanesia where ghosts exist among the living, equipped even with their own language (*talk blong tomate*), are given food (p. 161) and even places to sit (p. 163); there are young and old ghosts — it seems as if this is an alternative society, another dimension.

The ghosts of women who have died giving birth are the most powerful of all: they are seen as evil spirits, nameless, but referred to as *tomate pa na savo* (the ghosts of the confining house). They were feared because it was felt that they dragged other women to the fate they had experienced. Ange Mate was the most powerful of these ghosts and feared by the men because she forces them to have sex with her, the after-effects of which are 'a disappearing penis'. It is another example of death and sex being closely entwined, and — just like the nurse accused of castrating Telford — of women being seen as sexually predatory.

The ghosts are also a link with the past: they remind us of what we have lost, and Rivers eventually reflects on how they (the spirits) viewed it on the island, and he asks himself if they were offended by it. It is a surprising acceptance by a scientist that such an extra dimension of experience and understanding can exist.

The title of the novel is a reference to an extended metaphor that runs throughout the whole novel: all the characters — and by extension all of us — are ghosts travelling on a road to their own fate; they are living ghosts, either made dead by their experiences, or just waiting to die. It is a grim, fatalistic image that points towards the inevitability of the destination.

Skulls

How we view death often tells us something about how we view life: for Rivers, who was an anthropologist, such a statement would be obvious. Both he and Prior move between the fault lines of society, commenting on different cultural and social perspectives, noticing and analysing the differences. Connections are often made, and others are left to the reader to make. When Rivers notices that Mrs Irving, his landlady, has built a small shrine to her dead son he thinks about the connections between the two cultures: 'A shrine. Not fundamentally different from the skull houses of Pa Na Gundu where he'd gone with Njiru. The same human impulses at work. Difficult to know what to make of these flashes of cross-cultural recognition.'

It is Rivers's job to make such connections: the skull, the head, represents everything that he and Njiru value in their societies, but for different reasons. The tribes of Melanesia were head-hunters: the skull had a totemic power for them, symbolising as it did the ultimate appropriation of the enemy's power. Skulls are revered in Melanesia: they are stored, kept in what is effectively a shrine to them. For Njiru, who is descended from the greatest head-hunter of all, and for Rivers, the psychoanalyst, the skull — 'this blown eggshell' — contains everything vital to life. For Rivers it is a miracle, and for Njiru it is sacred because it 'contained the spirit, the *tomate*'. For both men the skull symbolises 'the highest value in the world'. It is a skull that stares at Rivers as he contemplates Hallet's injury (p. 230), and it is by considering the fate of the young soldier that we can make these cultural connections and see what values a society places upon this fragile container of life. In Western Europe such a precious object is treated with appalling brutality: Prior does his best to brush off parts of Hallet's brain, and every day men were dying in a casual extermination that still numbs. Barker's message seems to be clear: we condemned those, like Njiru, who head-hunted, and even made this way of life illegal, but how much superior are we who created the Somme, Ypres, Loos?

Language and structure

There is no doubt that some of the language — and the scenes it describes — are shocking, and deliberately so. How successful you think it is depends, to a great extent, on whether you think this is gratuitous or integral to the power of the action. Barker is attempting to convey difficult, conflicting and sometimes base emotions, and she often does that through Prior. He, more than any other character, is able to bridge the divide between the dirty and prosaic world of the street and the trenches, and the more elevated, respectable and dignified world of the officer class and the hospital. He acts as a conduit, or orifice, between the two, regularly puncturing the veneer of respectability with coarse but brutally honest observations and thoughts. For instance, he observes a gathering of a local religious group and wonders to himself 'how's the fucking?', and there are other examples of his voice conflicting with the (possibly) received notion that the soldiers at the Front, although admittedly placed in positions of extreme hardship, nevertheless retained a basic, simple, honest decency. Prior's use of language, the thoughts he expresses to himself, and the encounters he experiences, are used by Barker to show that the reality was conceivably very different — and far less sanitised and romantic — than we might allow ourselves to admit to on Remembrance Day.

There are two obvious lapses in the historical accuracy of Barker's use of English: on p. 109 Prior, mockingly, talks of 'lurve', which the Oxford English Dictionary (OED) cites as being first used in this sense in 1937; and on p. 156 Hocart, in response to a question by Rivers, says 'whatever', a usage which the OED defines as 'implying passive acceptance or tacit acquiescence…more pointedly to express indifference', and dates the first use to 1973. Barker seems to be saying that she deliberately writes in a more modern vernacular in order to break down preconceptions of the past: film makers do the same all the time when they set a film in the past, and we do not think twice about whether or not this compromises their message. Should it be different for novelists? To some extent, yes, because for the most part the author does attempt to stay close to the **tone** and register of the period and the different classes: Rivers does not use modern-day slang, and the two examples given add very little to the narrative, or the characters themselves. By inserting them Barker injects an unnecessary distraction which jars with the rest of the novel. There is a difference between avoiding archaic terms and using anachronisms.

This fusing of polarised ideas or concepts is extended to Barker's use of two very different locations: Melanesia and England. There are many links between the two cultures, and Barker wants us to focus on how similar they are, despite the obvious differences. Both cultures are facing profound upheavals, for very different reasons, but Barker concentrates particularly on the crisis in masculinity that is redefining what it means to be a man in each society. Killing is relative: the numbers do not really matter once it has become acceptable to achieve certain ends through force. So killing 20 native Melanesians, out of a population of, say, one or two hundred is just as catastrophic for that society as the Somme was for the British. What both locations show is how dependent we are on our contexts for making sense of the world, but Rivers demonstrates that we are better able to see the universality of human experience if we are able to compare and contrast our individual experiences. Njiru would be seen as a witch doctor by many in the West, but Rivers describes him as 'a good doctor' on p. 52 because he cares for his patients. It is Rivers who moves between these two worlds, sharing his experiences, adding different insights, and viewing each in, for the most part, a non-judgemental way. He is the observer, an objective viewer of change, and some might say a voyeur. The dual focus of the novel is essential to understanding the universality of the human condition: we feel the same things, even though we try to articulate them, and make sense of them, using different tools.

The opening chapter

The description of the 'Bradford businessmen', as well as **dialect** ('Ma-a-am', 'our Louie') immediately places the novel in the north of England. The opening location is the seaside, but this is no holiday idyll. The characters described are to some extent grotesques, being variously fat, balding, swollen, vulgar and cruel. Pain is inseparable from life in this world: sand grinds against flesh, skin burns in the sun, turning 'lobster-coloured'. It is a place of exposure, where people squint in the sun, visible and vulnerable, where children are referred to as 'it', and where a casual brutality pervades the atmosphere. It is also clear that the main character, Billy Prior, is more than a casual observer: for Louie, the young mother, he is a 'predator', and she is the prey: she sees him looking at her with 'blatant' lust.

Barker's narrative voice is very close to Billy Prior's here (indeed, at times they are indistinguishable, such as when Prior thinks to himself 'my God, he'd be regretting it tomorrow'). Prior is excluded from everyday sociable acts, such as sunbathing and holidaying with his family; he judges the people he is watching, noticing their class, their awkwardness when challenged by his rank. The language is direct and explicit ('hot spunk trickling down the thigh'), and after only two pages we feel that the subject matter is going to be dealt with in a gritty, realistic way, with each experience rendered as authentic as possible. The main themes seem to be class, sex, generational conflict, life and death. Prior sees Louie as a victim of her sex: pregnant when young, alone without the father of her child, condemned to returning against her will to live with her mother, and denied even the sense of responsibility that being a mother might usually bestow because it is taken from her (with perhaps both resentment and relief) by her mother. She is caught between two worlds: adulthood and childhood.

Details matter in this novel: we can tell what 'sort' she is by the fact that she smokes Woodbines, travels by bus, slaps her child, and wears make-up on the beach. She looks common, and to her mother this is an object of shame, but to Prior, being officer class, it is filled with a sexual charge: he sees her as 'gloriously, devastatingly, *fuckably* common', and it is this jolting vulgarity that makes us consider how sex and class have come together in these opening pages to suggest that they can both be used by the strong to repress and exploit the weak. But on the surface conventional modes of behaviour continue: Louie's mother calls Billy 'Sir', they exchange some very British niceties about the weather, and he touches his cap out of respect. Yet beneath the surface a range of powerful emotions are barely contained.

Like many novelists, Barker explores her themes through a succession of tensions. Innocence and experience, masculinity and femininity, working class and officer class, war and peace, health and illness — these and others are closely and skilfully juxtaposed. The encounter between Prior and the two women on the beach quickly establishes that sex will be a major theme in *The Ghost Road*, and as Prior continues his journey this is further developed. Innocence and experience are threaded through the passage, and Barker also employs colour **imagery** to represent the sensuous nature of remembrance. For instance, Prior's voyeuristic watching of a young man and woman is brought to an immediate halt when he notices her yellow skin: this presumably recalls a memory of the gassed casualties in the trenches, and with this image comes the 'automatic flow of bile', so strong that he has to turn away. It is at this point that a young child notices the man, 'so still among the swirl of dazzle', an outsider figure who, even though he smiles at her, carries an element of threat that the child responds to by holding on to her mother's skirt ('very wise' thinks Prior to himself). Innocence is everywhere and although Prior is viewed as a rather dark and threatening presence he is not unreceptive to it.

Prior is obviously divided in himself: he questions why he went to war instead of remaining at home working in a munitions factory (thus revealing to the reader that although he is an officer he is also working class) or taking a desk job in Whitehall. The fact that he turned each down suggests something complex about Prior because his decision to fight was not, as he admits, done out of a sense of duty. The sight of the lovers sets off a train of memories about his childhood, which continues the theme of generational conflict as he recalls how strict his father was with him. Each of these scenes establishes the style that the novel is going to be written in: Barker uses Prior to explore key themes through memory and association, and although it is written in the third person there is sometimes no distinction between the author's voice and that of the central character.

Prior seems to be a predatory male character, but it would be a mistake to see him only in this way. The fact that he has a complex set of emotions shows that there is more to him than sexual threat; indeed, by the time we get to p. 9 we begin to think that the conditions he has grown up in may explain why he is such an outsider. As an officer dressed in uniform he conveys a very definite set of preconceived masculine values, but these are undermined almost immediately with reference to Wilfred Owen, the war poet famed for his powerful verse as well as his bravery and, to some extent, his homosexuality. This sexual ambiguity is alluded to later on when Prior addresses himself, rather camply, as 'duckie', and claims he can 'always split in two', suggesting a divided personality and possibly even bisexuality. Prior's encounter with the doctor, Mather, develops the theme of sexual threat, as he pushes and 'jabs' his fingers into Prior's anus.

We also learn that Prior was sent home from France with shell shock. His recuperation, at Netley and Craiglockhart, meant that he was out of action from April to November, but at this time the asthma (which is described so graphically later in the novel) returns more regularly, suggesting that it is brought on by psychological rather than physical stimuli. Prior is no coward — he wishes to return to the Front, even though Mather suggests he might have done his bit — and he wishes to do so in order to escape civilians and their 'glib talk', but we are left wondering about the real reasons for him seeking to leave England. Homosexuality was decriminalised in the United Kingdom in 1967 but was still illegal in the British armed services until 1999. To a great extent homosexual behaviour was seen as unmasculine and damaging to morale; but in this novel (and in the previous two books in the trilogy) it is seen as something that is inevitable, given the close proximity of so many men living together in conditions of extreme intimacy and vulnerability. Masculinity is ambiguously presented in the opening chapter of this novel: Owen is described as being in love with Sassoon, but such emotions are not seen as being at odds with what is conventionally termed 'bravery'; indeed, history bears this out as Owen was awarded the MC and Sassoon the VC for bravery.

Barker is not interested in adopting a faux early twentieth-century writing style: the past is rendered as modern because it is described by an author who self-consciously wishes to avoid imitating contemporary technique. In an interview she said that writers

> …have to be historically accurate but very very careful not to put people off by any obviously archaic expression which makes them feel that this person who is speaking is somebody very different from me because the truth is he probably is not very different from you.

In other words, a modern writer has to show us that the subjects of the past remain perennially relevant, and accepting that allows us to place our own concerns into some sort of perspective. We have to ask ourselves, however, if the truth of the text becomes in turn almost self-validating because it is able to adopt a sense of enduring integrity: in other words, these themes are seen as worthwhile areas for a novelist to explore because they are seen to be fundamental to human experience (and even to the human condition). The reality could be that this is a borrowed profundity, and that these themes are the concerns of a modern audience, rather than those of the time in which the text is set. Barker acknowledged this:

> ...the historical novel really forces you to ask yourself all the time what is there in human nature that doesn't change, because that is what you have to write about because otherwise nobody is interested in reading what you have written anyway.
>
> 'A backdoor into the present: an interview with Pat Barker' by Wera Reush

Billy Prior strikes us as being a very modern character, preoccupied as he is with his own emotions, his motivations, his sexuality, and his relationships with others. Other characters, most notably Rivers, render the past as something very modern because their experiences are internalised and mediated through distinctly modern ideas (such as psychoanalysis). That said, Barker is conscious that by setting the book in the First World War there is enough of a critical distance to make it more interesting than a book, concerned with the same themes, set only a few years ago. As she has said, 'the pitfall about writing about the recent past is that nothing is more dead than yesterday or more irrelevant than last year's news'. This conflict continues to be relevant, as well as fascinating, to a modern reader and, inevitably, writers gain something from this effect.

Literary terms and concepts

The terms and concepts below have been selected for their relevance to talking and writing about *The Ghost Road*. It will aid argument and expression to become familiar with them and to use them in your discussion and essays.

allegory	extended metaphor that veils a moral or political underlying meaning
antithesis	contrasting of ideas by balancing words or phrases of opposite meaning; *The Ghost Road* is structured around a series of antitheses: masculine and feminine, war and peace, heterosexual and homosexual, the conscious and the unconscious
archetype	original model or idea used as a recurrent symbol: Billy Prior is an archetypal rebel or non-conformist who symbolises the clash of classes in the novel
belle époque	French for 'beautiful era', a period lasting approximately from the end of the Franco-Prussian War (1871) to the outbreak of the First World War (1914); characterised by relative political stability between nations and a flourishing of high culture

caricature	exaggerated and ridiculous portrayal of a person built around a specific physical or personality trait. Nellie, the prostitute, is a caricature of the working-class 'working girl'
cliché	predictable and overused expression or situation
colloquial	informal language of conversational speech
connotations	associations evoked by a word, e.g. 'flat 'suggests dull and uninteresting; skulls in *The Ghost Road* have both negative and positive connotations, being symbolic of both life (for Rivers and Njiru) and death (for Prior)
contextuality	historical, social and cultural background of a text; *The Ghost Road* has several contexts: Rivers's hospital, Melanesia, the battlefields of France; there is also the context in which Barker wrote it, as well as the context it is read and studied in
criticism	evaluation of literary text or other artistic work
defamiliarisation	making readers perceive something freshly by using devices that draw attention to themselves or by deviating from ordinary language and conventions. The passages set in Melanesia defamiliarise Western behaviour, forcing the reader to reassess accepted social conventions
dialect	variety of a language used in a particular area, distinguished by features of grammar and/or vocabulary, e.g. Ada Lumb's use of language on p. 70 ('By heck...', 'You're never thinking...', 'our Sarah' are examples of dialect from the north of England)
dialogue	direct speech of characters engaged in conversation
diction	choice of words; vocabulary from a particular semantic field, e.g. religion
dramatic irony	when the audience knows something the character speaking does not, which creates humour or tension; an obvious example is the inclusion of Wilfred Owen in the novel — we know his fate, and his nickname of 'the Ghost' (p. 180) is an example of dramatic irony
elegy	lament for the death or permanent loss of someone or something
empathy	identifying with a character in a literary work
epiphany	sudden and striking revelation of the essence of something sublime, e.g. Rivers's realisation (pp. 238–39) about the importance both Western and Melanesian cultures place on the skull.
eternal verities	fundamental and permanent truths of human existence

euphemism	tactful word or phrase to refer to something unpleasant or offensive
figurative	using imagery; non-literal use of language
form	the way a text is divided and organised, the shape of a text on the page; *The Ghost Road*'s form is intricately structured, and much of its power comes from its movement between the two different cultures (Europe and Melanesia), the past and the present, and the first and third person narratives
Freudian	reference to the belief of the Austrian psychoanalyst that early childhood experience affects all adult responses to life through the workings of the subconscious, where repressed urges lurk and reveal themselves in dreams and through 'Freudian slips'
genre	type or form of writing with identifiable characteristics, e.g. fairy tale
idiolect	style of speech peculiar to an individual character and recognisable as such
imagery	descriptive language appealing to the senses; imagery may be sustained or recurring throughout texts, usually in the form of simile or metaphor
irony	language intended to mean the opposite of the words expressed; or amusing or cruel reversal of an outcome expected, intended or deserved; situation in which one is mocked by fate or the facts
juxtaposition	placing side by side for (ironic) contrast of interpretation
metafiction	fictional construct that self-consciously and ironically exposes the devices of fiction
metaphor	suppressed comparison implied not stated, e.g. the prostitutes used by Wyatt ('dipping his wick where many a German wick has dipped before it', p. 245) are an obvious metaphor for France itself
Modernism	artistic movement rejecting previously accepted forms of expression that developed out of the First World War
motif	recurring verbal or structural device that reminds the audience of a theme, e.g. ghosts are used repeatedly throughout the novel to symbolise death in a variety of contexts
narrative	connected and usually chronological series of events that form a story; there are several narratives in *The Ghost Road*: Rivers's exploration of Melanesian culture, Prior's story, and the interaction between the two central characters

paradox	self-contradictory truth
pathetic fallacy	attributing emotions to inanimate objects, usually elements of nature, to represent the persona's feelings, e.g. the 'brutal, bloody disc' (p. 116) that Rivers observes is an extension of the warfare he and his country is involved in
persona	created voice within a text playing the role of narrator/speaker
personification	human embodiment of an abstraction or object, using capital letter or he/she; it could be argued that the French farm boy (p. 247) who is used by both German and British soldiers personifies France itself; Njiru personifies the culture of his tribe; and to some extent Rivers personifies the new, rationalist and enquiring mind of the twentieth century
plot	cause-and-effect sequence of events caused by characters' actions
plurality	possible multiple meanings of a text
postmodernism	contemporary literary movement, beginning around 1950
semantics	the study of meaning in language and communication
stereotype	a category of person with typical characteristics, often used for mockery; it could be argued that Prior's father is a stereotypical blunt working man who has a dislike of his more effete son
style	selection and organisation of language elements, related to genre or individual user of language
symbol	object, person or event which represents something more than itself; in *The Ghost Road* skulls symbolise life and death, snakes could be interpreted as phallic symbols
synopsis	summary of plot
syntax	arrangement of grammar and word order in sentence construction
theme	abstract idea or issue explored in a text
tone	emotional aspect of the voice of a text, e.g. 'bitter', 'exuberant'

Essay questions

Exam essays

You may be studying *The Ghost Road* for an examination or for coursework, but in both cases you need to know exactly which Assessment Objectives are being tested by your exam board and where the heaviest weighting falls. You will probably have looked at or practised specimen or past-paper questions so that you know what kind of title to expect, and it would be helpful if your teacher shared with you examiners' reports or notes for previous years' exams. Close reference to text is required even in closed text exams, and as quotation demonstrates 'use of text' it is often the most concise way of supporting a point. You are, however, more likely in a closed text exam to be set a general question dealing with structural or generic issues, theme or characterisation, often based on a critical comment. Even in an open-book exam the best-performing students do not need to refer to their text very often, so do not be intimidated if you are sitting a closed book exam.

Essay questions fall into the following categories: close section analysis and relation to whole text; characterisation; setting and atmosphere; structure and effectiveness; genre; language and style; themes and issues. With the introduction of the new specifications from 2008 there is also a 'creative/transformational' option available in the AQA A specification. Remember, however, that themes are relevant to all essays, and that analysis, not just description, is always required in questions that do not have an explicitly creative focus. Exam essays should be clearly structured, briskly argued, concisely expressed, closely focused, and supported by brief but constant textual references. They should show a combination of familiarity, understanding, analytical skill and informed personal response. Length is not in itself an issue — quality matters rather than quantity — but you have to prove your knowledge and fulfil the assessment criteria, and without sufficient coverage and exploration of the title you cannot be awarded a top mark. Aim realistically for approximately 12 paragraphs or four sides of A4.

Do not take up one absolute position and argue only one interpretation. There are no 'yes' or 'no' answers in literature. The other side must have something to be said for it or the question would not have been set, so consider both views before deciding which one to argue, and mention the other one first to prove your awareness of different reader opinions and audience reactions. It is permissible to say your response is equally balanced, provided that you have explained the contradictory evidence and have proved that ambivalence is built into the text.

Exam essay process

The secret of exam essay success is a good plan, which gives coverage and exploration of the title and refers to the four elements of text: **plot**, characterisation, language and themes. Think about the issues freshly rather than attempting to regurgitate your own or someone else's ideas, and avoid giving the impression of a pre-packaged essay you are determined to deliver whatever the title.

When you have chosen a question, underline its key words and define them briefly, in as many ways as are relevant to the text, to form the introduction and provide the background. Plan the rest of the essay, staying focused on the question, in approximately 12 points, recorded as short phrases and with indication of evidence. Include a concluding point that does not repeat anything already said but pulls your ideas together to form an overview. It may refer to other readers' opinions, refer back to the title, or include a relevant quotation from the text or elsewhere.

Check your plan to see that you have dealt with all parts of the question, have used examples of the four elements of text in your support, and have analysed, not just described. Remind yourself of the Assessment Objectives (printed on the exam paper). Group points and organise the plan into a structure with numbers, brackets or arrows.

Tick off the points in your plan as you use them in the writing of your essay, and put a diagonal line through the whole plan once you have finished. You can add extra material as you write, as long as it does not take you away from the outline you have constructed.

Concentrate on expressing yourself clearly as you write your essay, and on writing accurately, concisely and precisely (e.g. 'the long vowel sounds create a mournful effect' is more specific than 'it sounds sad'). Integrate short quotations throughout the essay.

Allow five minutes at the end for checking and improving your essay in content and style. Insertions and crossings-out, if legible, are encouraged. As well as checking accuracy of spelling, grammar and punctuation, watch out for errors of fact, name or title slips, repetition, and absence of linkage between paragraphs. Make sure your conclusion sounds conclusive, and not as though you have run out of time, ink or ideas. A few minutes spent checking can make the difference of a grade.

Planning practice

It is a useful class activity to play at being examiners and to set essay titles in groups and exchange them for planning practice. This makes you think about the main issues, some perhaps not previously considered, and which episodes would lend themselves as support for whole-text questions.

Using some of the titles below, practise planning essay titles within a time limit of eight minutes, using about half a page. Aim for at least ten points and know how you would support them. Use numbers to structure the plan. Get used to using note form and abbreviations for names to save time, and to either not using your text (for closed-book examinations) or using it as little as possible.

Since beginnings are the most daunting part of an essay for many students, you could also practise opening paragraphs for your planned essays. Remember to define the terms of the title, especially any abstract words, and this will give your essay breadth, depth and structure, e.g. if the word 'wartime' appears, say exactly what you take 'wartime' to mean, and how it applies to the novel you have studied.

Students also find conclusions difficult, so experiment with final paragraphs for the essays you have planned. The whole essay is working towards the conclusion, so you need to know what it is going to be before you start writing the essay, and to make it clear that you have proved your case.

Exam questions

General questions

1 To what extent would you agree that the literature of war reasserts mankind's essential goodness, rather than his willingness to destroy? Comment on and analyse the connections between *at least two* texts you have studied in the light of this observation.

2 To what extent would you agree that war literature asserts a sense of mankind's dignity in his attempt to assert a sense of order in a universe that seems chaotic? Comment on and analyse the connections between *at least two* texts you have studied in the light of this observation.

3 To what extent would you say that war literature allows us, perhaps more than anything else, to keep a 'chain of experience intact', and in doing so permits us to see both the best and worst of human nature?

4 'The writer's task is to turn everything inside out and upside down in order to make us reconsider the evidence of our eyes.' Comment on and analyse the connections and comparisons between *at least two* texts you have studied in the light of this claim.

5 'War is never an old subject because each new writer and each new reader finds something new.' Comment on and analyse the connections between *at least two* texts you have studied in the light of this observation.

6 'War strips away the skin of respectability: what it sees underneath is often society's true self.' Comment on and analyse the connections between *at least two* texts you have studied in the light of this observation.

7 'Writers — if they are doing their jobs correctly — must be anti-war.' Comment on and analyse the connections between *at least two* texts you have studied in the light of this observation.

8   Wilfred Owen once wrote that: 'My subject is war, and the pity of war. The poetry is in the pity.' Would you agree that this is the only subject matter for a writer who is concerned with war? Comment on and analyse the connections between *at least two* texts you have studied in the light of this observation.

9   'In any literature concerned with war it is invariably the case that female characters are portrayed as victims and male characters are the abusers.' Comment on and analyse the connections between *at least two* texts you have studied in the light of this observation.

10 'No writer can ever truly convey the horror of war.' Comment on and analyse the connections between *at least two* texts you have studied in the light of this observation.

In your responses to the above questions you must ensure that at least one text is a post-1990 text, and you should demonstrate what it means to be considering texts as a modern reader, in a modern context, and that other readers at other times may have had other responses.

Text-specific questions

1   How does Barker's structuring of *The Ghost Road* affect your interpretation of the novel?

2   Comment on the presentation of masculinity in *The Ghost Road*.

3   To what extent are the characters in *The Ghost Road* victims of their own gender?

4   Would you agree that *The Ghost Road* sees nothing hopeful about the modern human condition?

5   Compare and contrast the presentation of Rivers and Prior: which character in your view presents the most illuminating insight into the human condition at the beginning of the twentieth century?

6   Discuss the presentation of love in *The Ghost Road*.

7   Would you agree that Barker is as more interested in the psychological battlefield than the physical battlefield? Explain your answer with close reference to the text.

8   To what extent would you agree that Billy Prior is a character who is alienated from every context he finds himself in?

9   To what extent has Barker presented a new interpretation of the First World War? What do you think *The Ghost Road* contributes to our understanding of the conflict?

10 'In *The Ghost Road* sex is more to do with conflict and power than love and intimacy.' To what extent would you agree with this?

Specimen plan

Comment on the presentation of masculinity in *The Ghost Road*.

Possible plan

- There are different 'models': society determines what is masculine, and it does so, at its most extreme, in times of war.
- Femininity becomes **stereotyped** as well: it is caring, protective, and often passive.
- Barker seeks to challenge our view of masculinity: what does it mean to be a 'man'? What passes for conventional male behaviour in this context: fighting, becoming engaged, having sex with a woman, seeking adventure…
- Discuss how these events are presented; none of these seem either fulfilling or innate.
- Prior is central to any analysis and the focus should be on his challenging orthodox views of what this 'quality' means: sexually mobile, predatory, brave (but possibly delusional), a leader of men, but also an exploiter of men as well.
- Other models would include Rivers: he displays what could be termed characteristically 'feminine' qualities; the natives of Melanesia who are 'emasculated' by being stopped from head-hunting, the various minor characters who fight alongside Prior, or who are patients of Rivers.
- Focus on key passages: look at Prior interacting with both male and female characters, socially and sexually: when is he most 'masculine'? What is Barker's point?
- Is she seeking to deconstruct such outmoded terms (outmoded perhaps for the modern reader, rather than those characters and times it is describing)? Or is she asking us to widen or redefine our definitions?

Sample essays

Sample essay 1

Barker's subject is not the conflict of the trenches but the 'hidden battlefront' of the mind. After studying *The Ghost Road* to what extent would you agree with this?

The very fact that much of the novel is set in a psychiatric hospital, rather than the trenches, shows us where Barker wishes to focus as a writer. A psychological understanding of experience is at the core of the novel: we learn about the First World War and the traumatic effects it had on all the characters in their different ways, especially Billy Prior, the protagonist in the novel. However, Barker ensures that we experience the physical, which is integral to the novel because it enables the psychological to exist and shape our understanding of the war. The hospital in Craiglockhart, where the novel is largely (but not exclusively) set, is as much a battleground as the trenches of Northern France, the place where they fought for their lives.

The study of the mind is a key aspect of the novel because Barker focuses on the perceptual as well as the physical. She employs psychoanalytical ideas throughout to explore the deterioration and recovery of personality. William Rivers, the factual character in the novel, is interested in the relation between mind and body. The battlefront exists within the mind, but it is created in the physical conditions of man, be this the hospital or the trench. Barker refers to it as the 'hidden battlefront of the mental hospital' and it is easy to see why. Psychoanalysis is a form of psychotherapy developed by Sigmund Freud. Freud diagnosed and treated people with mental and emotional disorders and Barker employs many of his claims (with Rivers as the means for doing this) in order to explore psychosis. Towards the end of part one of the novel, when Prior is talking to Rivers about going back to the front, he says, 'you don't think I should be going back at all'. Rivers asks if Prior remembers 'saying something to me once about the ones who go back b-being the real test cases?' In other words, Barker — through Rivers — is asking us to consider what constitutes sanity and insanity in this context: are those who wish to 'do their duty' mad? Or are they quite sane? It is, a catch-22, and there are conscious echoes here of Heller's earlier novel.

Soldiers were physically damaged by what they experienced, but it was their minds that became the No Man's Land of the war, a place soon occupied by doctors and poets, each concerned with loss: loss of innocence, loss of life and, to some extent, loss of masculinity.

Masculinity in this novel is inseparable from class. The First World War marked the beginning of a new social order, a time when inherited respect was no longer to be easily assumed by the ruling classes. Society would be divided as never before. At the beginning of the novel Barker comments on the 'intricate horror' of the English class system and this horror is ruthlessly explored by Prior: it is he who moves between each of the classes, and he does so out of self-interest — having sex with anyone from a working-class female prostitute to an upper-class male senior officer. Prior is defined by his class, yet there is a sense that he is also exploited by others, and characterised by the army as someone from an undesirable background. Indeed, class runs through the whole narrative. When Hallet's family 'stood up again' as Rivers arrives to talk to them about their son's tragic death he has to reassure them that it is not necessary for them to stand up. Yet they do so, indicating just how embedded such habits are: they are instinctive, and they rule societies at times of peace and in times of war. Class tears people apart and binds them together, and in the England of 1918 such barriers were rapidly disappearing.

It is not just British society which is explored by Barker: she also describes another culture in Melanesia, which helps to convey a hidden battlefront and the cultural and ethical issues it brings to the novel. Rivers went to Melanesia to make the first developments in cross-culture examination, comparing the extent of the similarities between the two cultures. In the novel he examines the similarities and differences between the cultures during the war. At one point Rivers admits that it is 'almost easier now to ask a man about his private life than to ask what beliefs he lived by...the change had started years before the war'.

It is as if the war has destroyed any moral compass to navigate either the individual or the society he or she lived in: the scars on the country were real and imagined, and they reached inside us as well as beyond the seas, shaping other cultures. During Rivers's time in Melanesia (which occurred before the war) we learn about how conflict affects any society it occurs in. For instance, when Njiru offers a prayer he says 'be propitious in war… and be propitious and smite our enemies' and this clarifies just how integral aggression is to this society. His people honour 'stone ghosts' which 'were erected as memorials to men who died and whose bodies could not be brought home', a direct parallel with the fallen of the First World War. Barker links the two cultures through war and peace, conflict and remembrance, and indeed we can gain a profound understanding of a society if we look at how it treats the imprisoned and the injured. When examining the life in Melanesia Rivers comments on 'the abrupt transition from ritual to everyday life' and this illustrates very well the psychological link with the trenches and civilian life. Such swift movement between the physical and the psychological, between the regimented and the informal, are as recognisably British as Melanesian, as are the inevitable breakdowns that occur. Such a focus on the psychological makes the reader consider what is worth preserving and defending. Njiru focused on the fact that a head is a 'blown eggshell' which 'contained the only products of the forces of evolution capable of understanding its own origins'.

No matter what culture you live in, mankind is able to reflect on itself and its place in the universe; Baker makes us consider the fragility of life and the imminence of death. Such reflection defines us as human.

Sample essay 2

Remind yourself of the passage in the novel which begins on p. 196 ('We got a rope underneath him') and ends on p. 198 ('I saw the setting sun rise'). Analyse Barker's language closely and consider the themes explored in this passage.

In this key passage Barker uses visceral language to show the psychological and physical impact of war on both the protagonist Billy Prior as well as the other soldiers. Through Prior, Barker explores major themes of life and death and duty and betrayal, using striking imagery to bring to life Billy Prior's personal hell. In adopting the first person narrative, as opposed to the third (in which the majority of the novel is written) Barker immediately intensifies the scenes described. This passage illustrates Prior's bravery in going 'over the top' to save a seriously wounded soldier. Normally these actions would seem very heroic; however, Prior's personal account seems to show that he is simply doing his duty, and nothing more: he does not reflect on being brave. The nature of that duty becomes problematic: why do something that only prolongs suffering (as here)? Barker asks us to consider how his thoughts reveal an understanding of the futility of war. His actions reveal a depth of despair, and this is emphasised through the language (with the inclusion of rhetorical questions such as 'what's the use? He's going to die anyway.' And 'Die can't you?'). Nevertheless, his thoughts and actions humanise Prior: outwardly he appears heroic, but the first person narrative allows us to see how unheroic his actions really are. Paradoxically, after reading about Prior's behaviour for much of the book, this conventional 'soldierly' action, remarkable as it is, is one of the most 'normal' things he does in the whole narrative, and it adds another dimension to him for the reader. However, it is not an act of straightforward heroism.

Prior admits that he 'thought about killing him' because he is now so surrounded by death that he no longer values life in a purely humane way. The tone Barker uses in this passage re-presents Prior because it gives him a distinct — and very personal — voice. There is a casualness to his observations, as well as a deliberately un-poetic series of images (for instance, he describes the sun as 'the sodding thing') which acts as a useful balance to the images we have all become used to from reading Owen, Sassoon, Thomas and others. This language is effective because it is so human, so modern, and so undemonstrative. This is a character who seems, for the most part, at home in a landscape that is almost Bosch-like in its horror, and this makes the final image all the more unsettling because it shocks a character who, until this point, appears to have become thoroughly inured to life's extremes.

The **syntax** of the passage is effective in allowing us to understand Prior's emotions. The short sentences heighten the rawness of the experience ('We fell into a trench. Hallet on top of us'). Such language is precise and reflects the immediacy of the situation: it is as if Prior is a correspondent filing copy for the newspaper at home. To some extent these short, blunt images show how Prior has become desensitised by trench life: they reveal that something as horrific as falling into a trench with a critically injured soldier on top of him has become usual. It is entirely convincing, and all the more powerful for avoiding sentimentality, which would have been at odds with the character.

This is another world, and we are not allowed to forget it. There are constant references to 'craters' and 'utter lifelessness', creating images of trench life being extra-terrestrial. Barker is highlighting how war is 'something that couldn't be happening on earth'. To emphasise the 'lifelessness' of war she writes that 'Even the crows have given up', an effective image because we associate crows with scavenging, with death, and with darkness. If *they* have given up, what chance has man got?

Hallet, the novel's personification of youthful, middle-class, ardent belief, is the inevitable victim in this conflict. It is he who effectively loses his life, but also it is he who represents the loss of optimism, and it had to be *him* who meets this fate because it is he — and his family — who are seen as the type who prolonged the war, who continued to believe in it when nobody else could. We see him in gruesome, unrelenting detail: we read of how Prior sees 'the fillings in his back teeth and his mouth filled with blood', something which makes him all the more vulnerable, all the more real. Barker continues to use colloquial language effectively; for example Prior notices 'a gob of Hallet's brain' between his fingers and finds himself 'brushing' it away, but the casual action of brushing something away is in striking contrast with the horror of the situation and what it is he is trying to rid himself of: he cannot shake off the true horror of what he holds. The use of the onomatopoeic 'gob' is highly effective, rendering something as sublime as the human brain

(and we will see this explored by Rivers and Njiru later on) as nothing more than a lump, a bit of texture, an inconvenience.

In this utterly changed landscape there appears to be nothing to cling to: no hope, no life and no God. In fact the language used by Prior seems to question the idea of God's existence; he says that 'too little mercy had been shown by either side for gestures of that sort to be possible' and in this context 'mercy' hints at the idea of forgiveness, or repentance, something which is also alien here. So what are we left with at the end of this passage? To some extent our expectations have been subverted: Prior, that difficult, uncompromising central character, appears, at first, to resort to being the stereotypical CO: he is prepared to rescue a soldier under his command, and in doing so risk his own life. But the reality is different: he questions the whole process and even wishes that Hallet would die. Furthermore, his action only highlights just how alienated mankind has become from his environment, and how nihilistic this new world is. The final image, of the setting sun rising, is suitably unsettling: time has been suspended and the natural order changed or reversed. Worse, 'there are no words' left to describe the emotions being felt. What we have instead is silence, and knowledge that what had been created was something utterly new, and profoundly dangerous. The battle of the Somme was the beginning of the modern world. The bloodiest of all centuries had begun.

Further study

There are many books about the First World War. A very good — and brief and accessible — history of the conflict is Norman Stone's *First World War: A Short History* (2008, Penguin).

There are many other resources for a student to make use of in researching the First World War. Below is a selective bibliography of texts that will aid you in understanding the complexities of the First World War:

Fiction, memoirs, poetry

Blunden, E. (1982) *Undertones of War*, Penguin.
Fitzgerald, F. S. (1955) *Tender is the Night*, Penguin.
Graves, R. (1960) *Goodbye to All That*, Penguin.
Gurney, I. (1982) *Collected Poems* (ed. P. J. Kavanagh), Oxford University Press.
Gurney, I. (1984) *War Letters* (ed. R. K. R. Thornton), Hogarth.
Hemingway, E. (1935) *A Farewell to Arms*, Penguin.
Hill, S. (1989) *Strange Meeting*, Penguin.
Jones, D. (1987) *In Parenthesis*, Faber.
Owen, W. (1963) *Collected Poems* (ed. with an introduction and notes by C. Day Lewis and a memoir by Edmund Blunden), Chatto & Windus.

Owen, W. (1967) *Collected Letters* (ed. Harold Owen and John Bell), Oxford University Press.

Remarque, E. M. (1987) *All Quiet on the Western Front* (trans. A. W. Wheen), Picador.

Sassoon, S. (1945) *Siegfried's Journey 1916–1920*, Faber.

Sassoon, S. (1961) *Collected Poems 1908–1956*, Faber.

Toynbee, P. (1954) *Friends Apart*, MacGibbon & Kee.

Histories and cultural studies

Anderson, B. (1983) *Imagined Communities*, Verso.

Bergonzi, B. (1965) *Heroes' Twilight*, Constable.

Bond, B. (ed.) (1991) *The First World War and British Military History*, Oxford University Press.

Brownlow, K. (1979) *The War, the West and the Wilderness*, Secker & Warburg.

Cannadine, D. (1984) 'Death, Grief and Mourning in Modern Britain', in Joachim Whalley (ed.), *Mirrors of Mortality*, Europa.

Capa, R. (1985) *Photographs* (eds Richard Whelan and Cornell Capa), Faber.

Clark, A. (1991) *The Donkeys*, Pimlico.

Dyer, G. (1994) *The Missing of the Somme*, Phoenix.

Ferro, M. (1973) *The Great War*, Routledge.

Foot, M. R. D. (1990) *Art and War*, Headline.

Fussell, P. (1975) *The Great War and Modern Memory*, Oxford University Press.

Hibberd, D. (1992) *Wilfred Owen: The Last Year*, Constable.

Hynes, S. (1992) *A War Imagined: The First World War and English Culture*, Pimlico.

Hynes, S. (1992) *The Auden Generation*, Pimlico.

Larkin, P. (1983) *Required Writing*, Faber.

Liddell Hart, B. H. (1970) *History of the First World War*, Cassell.

Macdonald, L. (1978) *They Called it Passchendaele*, Michael Joseph.

Macdonald, L. (1980) *The Roses of No Man's Land*, Michael Joseph.

Macdonald, L. (1987) *1914*, Michael Joseph.

Orwell, G. (1970) *The Collected Essays, Journalism and Letters, Vol. 1*, Penguin.

Parker, P. (1987) *The Old Lie: the Great War and the Public School Ethos*, Constable and Co.

Robbins, K. (1984) *The First World War*, Oxford University Press.

Stallworthy, J. (1974) *Wilfred Owen*, Oxford University Press.

Taylor, A. J. P. (1966) *The First World War*, Penguin.

Viney, N. (1991) *Images of Wartime*, David & Charles.

Whelan, R. (1985) *Robert Capa: A Biography*, Faber.

Winter, D. (1979) *Death's Men*, Penguin.

Young, J. E. (1993) *The Texture of Memory: Holocaust Memorials and Meaning*, Yale University Press.

Anthologies

Glover, J. and Silkin, J. (1990) *The Penguin Book of First World War Prose*, Penguin.

Macdonald, L. (1988) *1914–1918: Voices and Images from the Great War*, Michael Joseph.

Silkin, J. (ed.) (1981) *The Penguin Book of First World War Poetry* (2nd edn), Penguin.

Stallworthy, J. (1988) *The Oxford Book of War Poetry*, Oxford University Press.

Vansittart, P. (1981) *Voices from the Great War*, Cape.

Criticism

No books of **criticism** have yet been published on *The Ghost Road*. There are some interviews with Barker on the internet, but a good place to start browsing is the Contemporary Writers website: www.contemporarywriters.com/authors/ ?p=auth15. You can also find an interview with Barker here: http://muse.jhu.edu/ demo/contemporary_literature/v045/45.1nixon.html, and here: www.bbc.co.uk/ radio4/arts/openbook/openbook_20030831.shtml, although she talks about texts other than those in the *Regeneration* trilogy.

There are also a lot of websites dedicated to the conflict, but the BBC's site is extremely good and user-friendly: www.bbc.co.uk/history/worldwars/wwone/.

Other websites with information

For general reference:

www.britannica.com

en.wikipedia.org/wiki/Main_Page

For resources specific to the war:

www.nationalarchives.gov.uk/pathways/firstworldwar/index.htm

info.ox.ac.uk/jtap/

www.bbc.co.uk/religion/remembrance/poetry/wwone.shtml

Brigham Young University's First World War Literature

www.ww1photos.com/

www.firstworldwar.com/

www.iwm.org.uk/

Film version

The first part of Barker's trilogy — *Regeneration* — was made into a film in 1997. It was directed by Gillies MacKinnon, and starred Jonathan Pryce as Rivers and Jonny Lee Miller as Billy Prior. It was well received and was nominated for many awards.